The Secret Life of Walter Mitty

A Musical

Book by Joe Manchester
Lyrics by Earl Shuman
Music by James Thurber

*Based on the Classic Story
by Leon Carr*

A SAMUEL FRENCH ACTING EDITION

SAMUEL FRENCH

FOUNDED 1830

SAMUELFRENCH.COM
SAMUELFRENCH-LONDON.CO.UK

FOR PRODUCTION ENQUIRIES

UNITED STATES AND CANADA
Info@SamuelFrench.com
1-866-598-8449

UNITED KINGDOM AND EUROPE
Plays@SamuelFrench-London.co.uk
020-7255-4302

Each title is subject to availability from Samuel French, depending upon country of performance. Please be aware that *THE SECRET LIFE OF WALTER MITTY* may not be licensed by Samuel French in your territory. Professional and amateur producers should contact the nearest Samuel French office or licensing partner to verify availability.

STORY OF THE PLAY

Upon reaching his fortieth birthday, Walter Mitty, the James Thurber character whose name has become a household word, reflects on his rather drab, ordinary life. Defeated in his quest for wealth and glory by family responsibilities, a mortgage, a routine job, and his own propensity for dreaming rather than doing, Walter creates elaborate fantasies in which he, of course, is always the hero. His Secret World is so enticing that Walter often loses sight of the boundary between dream and reality and comically slips into the world of his imagination. An attractive would-be chanteuse aptly named Willa de Wisp encourages Walter to leave his nagging but devoted wife Agnes, to shed the burdens of suburban living, and really live The Secret Life. Unfortunately, however, The Secret Life is as unattainable as it is appealing, and through an amusing twist at the end of the play, Walter discovers to his own surprise that he is happily committed to the real world, complete with its mortgages and responsibilities.

Thurber's gentle wit and deep insight into the stresses and strains of the workaday world on the Little Man make an unexpectedly good basis for this fine musical treatment. The witty book is embellished with a fine score of tunes that capture the comedy (*Marriage Is for Old Folks; Two Little Pussycats*), the tenderness (*Aggie*), and the refreshing liveliness (*Confidence; Hello, I Love You, Goodbye*) that, according to TIME MAGAZINE, make *The Secret Life of Walter Mitty* "a thoroughly pleasant musical evening." Original cast album available on Columbia Records.

3

THE SECRET LIFE OF WALTER MITTY was first presented by Joe Manchester in association with J. M. Fried at the Players Theatre, New York City. The entire production was staged by Mervyn Nelson and starred Marc London, Cathryn Damon, Rue McClanahan, Eugene Roche and Lorraine Serabian.

CHARACTERS
(*In Order of Appearance*)

WALTER MITTY
MACMILLAN
FIRING SQUAD
PEASANT WOMEN
AGNES MITTY
PENINNAH MITTY
MISSION CONTROL OPERATOR (MacMillan)
SURGICAL PATIENT (MacMillan)
HEAD NURSE
DR. RENSHAW
DR. BENBOW
PROFESSOR REMINGTON
DR. PRITCHARD-MITFORD
FIRST NURSE
SECOND NURSE
HARRY
WILLA
IRVING
RUTHIE
FRED GORMAN
HAZEL
CRÊPE SUZETTE
TORTONI
APPLE TURNOVER
TOWNSPEOPLE
BLIND DATE
FOLIES CUSTOMERS
MALE DANCERS
GROUP THERAPY PATIENTS
SYLVIA

NOTE: A total of 15 actors were used in the original New York production, each one playing several roles. However, as many more actors as desired may be used in this show.

DESCRIPTION OF MAIN CHARACTERS

WALTER MITTY: He is 40. A whimsical, henpecked, dreamer supreme. Instantly likeable.

AGNES: Mitty's wife. Around 35. Reasonably attractive, nagging, practical, but underneath her strong veneer, she is sensitive, understanding and smart.

PENINNAH: Their daughter. Around 10, unspoiled, sweet.

HARRY: In his 40's. Pleasant, friendly bartender type.

WILLA: Late 20's, early 30's. She is a sexy and kookie night club singer.

IRVING: About 30, slightly dense. He is a stern believer in health foods and spas, and looks it.

RUTHIE. She is in her 20's. Volatile and a little on the crude side. Pretty in a cheap sort of way.

GORMAN: He is 40. A successful salesman type with a gift of gab and great charm.

HAZEL: Mid-20's, speaks with a lisp, dumb as they come.

SYLVIA: In her 20's. Definitely not the finishing school type.

MACMILLAN: Around 50. A large, pompous, gruff man.

TIME: The Present; Waterbury, Connecticut; Autumn.
ACTION: Takes place in the everyday and the secret life of Walter Mitty.

RUNNING ORDER AND MUSICAL NUMBERS

ACT ONE

Scene 1: PROLOGUE
THE SECRET LIFE #1
TAPOCKETA DREAM MUSIC #1A
THE WALTER MITTY MARCH #2

Scene 2: KITCHEN

Scene 3: SPACE DREAM
ASTRONAUT DREAM #2A

Scene 4: KITCHEN
WALKING WITH PENINNAH #3

Scene 5: SURGICAL DREAM
TAPOCKETA DREAM THEME #3A
DRIP, DROP, TAPOCKETA #4

Scene 6: KITCHEN
AGGIE #5
SCENE CHANGE #5A

Scene 7: AUTOMOBILE
DON'T FORGET #6
SCENE CHANGE #6A

Scene 8: HARRY'S BAR
MARRIAGE IS FOR OLD FOLKS #7
HELLO, I LOVE YOU, GOODBYE #8

Scene 9: PLAYBOY PENTHOUSE DREAM
STRIP #9

Scene 10: HARRY'S BAR
WILLA #10
CONFIDENCE #11
UNDERSCORING #11A

Scene 11: TELEPHONE SEQUENCE—FINALE
TELEPHONE NUMBER #12
THE NEW WALTER MITTY #13

ACT TWO

NOTE: See set plot in the back of the book for details on simplification of scene changes.

The Secret Life of Walter Mitty

ACT ONE

SCENE 1 (Prologue)

As the HOUSE LIGHTS dim to half, we hear Offstage CHORUS *sing:*

THE SECRET LIFE   *MUSIC CUE #1*

TENOR.
> When the world seems hard to bear,
> You can dream a dream,
> And suddenly you're there
> In the secret life, the secret life!
>
> Time goes by against your will,
> But just a dream away,
> Time is standing still
> In the secret life, the secret life!

CHORUS.
> From earthbound to boundless you fly,
>> (*HOUSE LIGHTS out. STAGE LIGHTS come up slowly to reveal* MITTY *shaving. He is in undershirt and shorts, behind scrim* U. R.)
>
> Tall, proud and free,
> To be all you long to be!
>
> And who's to know, and who's to say
> Which world is really real,
> The world of every day,
> Or the secret life, the secret life, the secret life,
> The secret life, the secret life.

(*TAPOCKETA THEME—#1A—direct segue from #1.*)

(*The SCRIM rises.* MITTY *suddenly stops shaving and stands motionless, pensive. Then, with a certain dignity, a certain*

9

aplomb, he marches to U. C. *and stands at attention. In a moment, FIRING SQUAD, led by* MacMillan, *enters* R., *along with several* Peasant Women, L. All *sing:*)

THE WALTER MITTY MARCH   *MUSIC CUE #2*

All.
> Walter Mitty! The greatest in the land!
> Walter Mitty! One man who takes a stand!
>
> Hail! Hail! Beloved foe,
> Everybody shout his praises!
> Tapocketa, Tapocketa, Tapocketa-pocketa, Tapocketa!
>
> Mighty Mitty! You're hist'ry's shining light,
> Walter Mitty! Hey man, you're out of sight!

(*MUSIC continues under dialogue.* MacMillan *takes position* R. *of* Mitty, *removes piece of rope from pocket, starts to tie* Mitty's *hands.*)

Mitty. Sir! (*Voluntarily puts hands behind his back as* Peasant Women *cry: "How brave!" "Mercy!" "What a mighty man!" etc.* MacMillan *throws rope away, removes blindfold from pocket and attempts to cover* Mitty's *eyes.*) To hell with the handkerchief! (*More cries from* Peasant Women.)

MacMillan. (*Unfolds scroll, reads:*) Walter Mitty, by my order, I, S.O.B. MacMillan, your employer, have found you guilty as charged and hereby sentence you to be shot! (Peasant Women *react.* MacMillan *offers* Mitty *a cigarette.*) Would you like a cigarette? (Mitty *shakes head "no," coughs and points to his congested chest.*) Have you any last request?

Mitty. If you don't mind, I'd like to give the final command myself.

(Peasant Women: *"Have you ever seen anything like it?" "What courage!" "My hero!" etc.*)

MacMillan. (*Impressed.*) As you wish. (*To* Squad.) Forward 'arch! (Squad *takes position in front of* Mitty. *MUSIC OUT. DRUM ROLL.*) Good luck, Mitty. (*They shake hands.*)

Mitty. (*Cool.*) Thank you. (MacMillan *steps aside as* Peasant Women *continue their cries and pleadings.* Mitty *draws a deep breath, then addresses* Squad.) Ready! Aim! (*Turns to* Peasant Women, *smiles confidently. To* Squad.) Right face! Forward 'arch!

(*MUSIC UP.* Squad *obeys command and exits* L., *along with* MacMillan. Mitty, *pleased with himself, is showered with flowers and kisses from* Peasant Women. *He laughs triumphantly as they throw themselves at his feet. MUSIC FADES as:*)

LIGHTS OUT

ACT ONE

Scene 2

LIGHTS up on Mitty Kitchen, a few seconds later. A Saturday morning in autumn. Agnes *is busy preparing breakfast;* Peninnah *sits at table, studying.*

Agnes. Walter! Walter J. Mitty! Can you hear me?

Mitty. (*Offstage.*) Huh? What did you say, Agnes?

Agnes. How many times am I going to ask you to come down to breakfast, Walter?

Mitty. (*Offstage.*) Oh, be right there, Agnes. Sorry, dear . . .

Agnes. (*Impatiently.*) Walter, I promised Gertrude we'd stop by. And I've got to go to the hairdresser. And today is Peninnah's accordion lesson. And you know I want to pick up a new timetable at the train station. Please hurry!

Peninnah. (*Looks up from book.*) Do you think Daddy will remember, Mommy?

Agnes. Remember what?

Peninnah. About today—his birthday!

Agnes. Well, if I know your father, probably not.

Peninnah. (*Rises, crosses to stairs.*) Oh, then maybe I better tell him!

Agnes. No, Peninnah. I think it's wise if we don't say anything. We'll just surprise him at dinner tonight when we bring out the cake and the presents.

Peninnah. All right. Okay. (*Crosses to cabinet.*)

Agnes. Walter!

Mitty. (*Offstage.*) Coming. Coming, dear.

Agnes. It never fails—everytime I have to go somewhere!

Peninnah. (*Removes small package from cabinet and crosses to* Agnes.) Look what I bought him from my allowance, Mommy. It's a pencil.

Agnes. That's very thoughtful.

Peninnah. It's not just a *pencil* pencil. It's the one that goes with the fountain pen I gave Daddy for his birthday last year. Now he'll have a set.

AGNES. I said that's very thoughtful, Peninnah. Now sit down and concentrate on your homework.

PENINNAH. (*Puts gift away, then crosses to table.*) I'm stuck on nimbus and cumulus clouds.

AGNES. Ask your father. I think he's stuck on them, too. That's what daddies are for. They know all about those things. (MITTY *appears* U. R., *crosses to chest of drawers, and proceeds to finish dressing.* AGNES *calls upstairs.*) Walter!

MITTY. Yes, dear? I'm hurrying.

AGNES. (*Impatiently.*) What's keeping you, Walter? You haven't eaten yet. The orange juice is getting warm and your coffee's getting cold. And you know what it's like to find a parking space at the station!

MITTY. (*Muttering to himself.*) Parking space at the station. By the time I'm forty, I'll have a chauffeur to park the car for me. By the time I'm forty, I'll be a millionaire, once or twice. (*Starts downstairs.*) But I've got to get started right away. Today!

AGNES. Walter!

MITTY. Well, tomorrow for sure. (*Enters kitchen area, kisses* AGNES *on cheek.*) G'morning, Agnes.

AGNES. It was a good morning when they hung Nathan Hale, too! (*Brushes* MITTY's *hair with her hand.*) Comb your hair back, Walter!

MITTY. (*Kisses* PENINNAH.) G'morning, Peninnah (Pen-EE-nah).

AGNES. Walter, Peninnah (Pen-EYE-nah)! You wouldn't believe it—his own daughter!

MITTY. (*Corrects himself.*) Peninnah. (*Lights cigarette.*)

AGNES. Walter!

MITTY. (*Takes puff.*) Yes, dear?

AGNES. Walter, are you smoking before breakfast? You know about your congested chest. After everything the *Reader's Digest* said about tobacco and your health—

MITTY. Oh, did the—

AGNES. —what reason would you have to smoke before breakfast?

MITTY. Just one, Agnes.

AGNES. People who smoke before breakfast are supposed to be tense, nervous and irritable.

MITTY. Oh, are they?

AGNES. (*Crosses to him, whips something in a bowl that makes annoying sound.*) Now what reason would you have to be tense, nervous or irritable before breakfast? (*He shrugs, turns ear away from annoying noise.*) Please put out that cigarette. (MITTY *starts to put it in ashtray on table.*) No, Walter! Not in Peninnah's ashtray. We want to save those. We don't use Peninnah's ashtrays. How are we going to follow her creative progression? Her teacher, Lillian Smalley—

PENINNAH. I made them all for you, Daddy!

AGNES. —told us to save her ashtrays.

MITTY. I know—but she made 23 last week alone!

AGNES. Here, give it to me—

MITTY. (*Asserting himself.*) Really now, Agnes, one cigarette can't hurt. Besides, it's an Astro.

AGNES. Astro?

MITTY. You know. With the space tip and double micronite filter and the long charcoal inserts—they don't have much room for tobacco!

AGNES. Well, hurry up and finish it. (MITTY *gazes at cigarette.*) Walter, wasn't there an article in the *Reader's Digest* recently about the Astro cigarette?

MITTY. What, Agnes? What?

AGNES. For heaven sakes, you're not even listening! I swear, if someone walked in here right now and saw you sitting like that, they'd think you were *on* something!

MITTY. On what, Agnes?

AGNES. Oh, what's the use! (*Handing him a banana.*) Walter, stop staring at that silly cigarette and slice this banana into your cereal and let's not have a lot of talking the first thing in the morning! (*Looks at watch.*) If I don't get my hair done on time, we'll never get to see Gertrude's new couch.

(MITTY *sits quietly, still gazing intently at his cigarette. In a moment,* PRIVATE MACMILLAN *appears* L. *with headphones and microphone.*)

MITTY. (*Barely audible.*) Don't worry, dear. I wouldn't want you to miss Gertrude's new couch . . . (*TAPOCKETA THEME into Astronaut Dream.*)

MUSIC CUE #2A

LIGHTS FADE

ACT ONE

SCENE 3

LIGHTS up on Astronaut Dream. MITTY *is wearing a space helmet;* PENINNAH *and* AGNES *continue as before.*

MACMILLAN. Commander Mitty? This is Operation Astro to Commander Mitty. Come in, Commander. Over and out.

MITTY. Space ship to Operation Astro. Commander Mitty speaking. Ready for blast-off from Mars. Holding couch-shaped-steel-belted-radial-rock specimen. Next stop, Earth.

MACMILLAN. If you're having trouble with the exhaust, Commander, we suggest you don't take any chances.

MITTY. The only time you're alive is when you take chances.

AGNES. He'll never make it.

PENINNAH. Daddy will make it all right. He always does, Mommy.

AGNES. Peninnah, don't interfere.

MACMILLAN. Commander, are you there?

AGNES. If he just sits there gazing we'll never get anywhere.

MACMILLAN. What's wrong, Commander?

MITTY. Tell the Old Man there's only one hope. I'm throwing on full throttle.

MACMILLAN. That's suicide!

MITTY. Well, we only live once, Private MacMillan. Or do we?

AGNES. And I want you to be sure to get overshoes for yourself. You know how susceptible you are to the flu.

MACMILLAN. Overshoes—? That static, Commander. Do you hear that static?

MITTY. Pressure shattering the coreopsis controls.

MACMILLAN. Do you know what it can be?

MITTY. Yes, but there's nothing you can do about it.

AGNES. Stop dreaming, Walter. I can't be late for the hairdresser. You know how furious Mr. Charles gets when any of us girls show up late. If you ever finish, we can get moving.

MACMILLAN. What's that? I can't hear you, Commander! We're getting interference as far as the Van Allen belt.

SPACE MUSIC UP

AGNES. The *Reader's Digest* says that this cereal is just packed with vitamins and minerals, Walter—

MACMILLAN. Go ahead, Commander. I think the interference is gone now. What are you going to do?

MITTY. I don't know. (*A beat.*) Hold it! My fountain pen— Peninnah's pen!

MACMILLAN. What's that, Commander?

MITTY. Shhh, quiet, you fool. (*Inserts pen in imaginary instrument panel.*) Ah, I was right—it cleared the exhaust—perfect! That will hold for ten minutes, just long enough to complete the first thrust and then start me off again!

MACMILLAN. (*Impressed.*) You are the most together man I have ever come across! God be with you, Commander.

MITTY. Thank you.

MACMILLAN. Count down:
Ten, nine, eight, seven, six, five,   *MUSIC OUT*
four, three, two, one, BLAST
OFF!   AGNES. (*Screams simultane-
                                                  ously   with   "Blast   off!"*)
                                                  Walter! Walter J. Mitty . . . !

BLACKOUT

ACT ONE

SCENE 4

LIGHTS quickly up on Mitty kitchen. AGNES is wiping banana from her face.

MITTY. Huh?

AGNES. You popped the banana right into my face! How could you?

PENINNAH. I'll find it. It went over there.

AGNES. (*To PENINNAH.*) Throw it in the garbage, Peninnah.

MITTY. It was an accident. Honest.

AGNES. There is no such thing as an accident!

MITTY. Yes there is. Of course there is.

AGNES. What is wrong with you, Walter? (PENINNAH *throws banana away, then crosses to* MITTY.)

PENINNAH. (*Pointing to his foot.*) Daddy, your sock is missing!

MITTY. (*Looks down.*) Oh, er, yes, I couldn't find the other one this morning, Peninnah (Pen-EE-nah).

AGNES. Pen-*eye*-nah!

MITTY. (*Corrects himself.*) Peninnah. You want to go upstairs like a good girl and see if it's hiding under something? (PENINNAH *crosses to stairs* R.)

AGNES. Just a moment, Peninnah. Stay where you are! (*To* MITTY.) Socks don't hide! Why don't you look and see if you put both on one foot?

MITTY. Now no one on earth would do a stupid thing like that. (*Checks, finds both socks on one foot.*)

AGNES. Ahah! (PENINNAH *holds back a snicker, then crosses* D. C.)

MITTY. Agnes, you're amazing—just amazing. You're the smartest wife— (*Voice trails off as he notices* AGNES *glaring at him.*)

AGNES. (*Clearing sink as* MITTY *takes off shoes and socks.*) Oh, by the way, Mr. MacMillan called. He wants you to be in tomorrow for inventory.

MITTY. (*Throws sock on table.*) On Sunday?

AGNES. Why don't you stand up and face him, Walter? (*Sarcastically.*) You'll have to do that before you get your own toy factory. Asking you to come in on Sunday! (*Notices sock on table, throws it on his lap.*) Take your sock off the table!

MITTY. I'm sorry.

AGNES. I don't know why anyone should take advantage of anyone who's worked so hard for his toy company. It's ridiculous. Gertrude's Eddie told his boss where to get off, and got a raise in return! And I certainly hope your inventory won't keep you from your daughter's first performance in the school health pageant.

MITTY. (*To* PENINNAH.) Nothing in the world could keep me away from that.

AGNES. Tell Daddy what you play.

MUSIC UP #3

PENINNAH. (*Crosses to* MITTY.) I play the "Spirit of Walk Around the Block Six Times a Day."

MITTY. I'll bet you're just perfect for that part! (*Stands, kisses her on cheek, then offers his arm which she grabs onto.*)

WALKIN' WITH PENINNAH

MITTY.
The skies are clearer when I'm walkin' with Peninnah,
The stars are nearer when I'm walkin' with Peninnah,
When she gives me that peanut butter smile,
Whatever mood I'm in, that sunny little grin
Makes life worth livin'.

My world is brighter when I'm walkin' with Peninnah,
My cares are lighter when I'm walkin' with Peninnah,
Some day she'll stray and wrinkle up my brow,
But I'm walkin' with Peninnah, my little Peninnah now.
PENINNAH.
The skies are clearer when I'm walkin' with my daddy,
The stars are nearer when I'm walkin' with my daddy,
When he gives me that Jack-O-Lantern smile,
My heart begins to hum, I suddenly become, a real live princess.

MITTY.

My world is brighter when I'm walkin' with Peninnah,
My cares are lighter when I'm walkin' with Peninnah,
Someday she'll stray and wrinkle up my brow,
But I'm walkin' with Peninnah,

PENINNAH.

My world is brighter when I'm walkin' with my daddy,
My cares are lighter when I'm walkin' with my daddy,

I'm walkin' with my daddy,

BOTH.
We're walkin' together now.

(MITTY *and* PENINNAH *sit at table* L. *as* AGNES *continues serving breakfast.*)

AGNES. Peninnah, close the book now and finish your breakfast.
PENINNAH. (*To* AGNES.) In a second. (*To* MITTY.) Daddy, what do anthracite coal and glucose have to do with each other?
MITTY. What do anthracite and—where do they ask a question like that, Peninnah?
PENINNAH. Here. Question 9.
MITTY. (*Hesitates.*) Are you sure that's the right book for your grade?
PENINNAH. (*Holds up book.*) Yes, Daddy. General Knowledge.
MITTY. Hmmm.
AGNES. (*Crosses to him, confidentially.*) Don't frustrate the child, Walter. Tell her. You know what Miss Smalley says—
PENINNAH. Miss Smalley says we should ask our parents if we're not sure.
MITTY. Well, Peninnah (Pen-EE-nah)—-
AGNES. Peninnah (Pen-EYE-nah)!
MITTY. (*Corrects himself.*) Peninnah. (*Stammering.*) There's a very definite relationship between glucose and anthracite coal. They're both underground—and—uh—things underground generally have a great deal in common, like roots of trees—uh—worms—gophers—and fish—- (*Considers.*) Underwater, of course! (*Relieved.*) And that's what anthracite and glucose coal have to do with each other.
PENINNAH. Gee, Daddy, I can't write all that. I'd better look it up.
MITTY. (*Incredulous.*) Look it up? You mean you have the answer?
PENINNAH. Yes, in the back of the book. (*Finds answer.*)
MITTY. (*After a beat.*) What does it say?
PENINNAH. It says "nothing." They've got nothing to do with each other! (*Chuckles.*)
MITTY. (*Defensively.*) Oh, well—that's the way it often is in nature. Take your mother and me, for instance—-

AGNES. (*Turns on him.*) Walter, that's not funny!

MITTY. (*Rises.*) Sorry. I'll go back the car out.

AGNES. (*Takes coat, bag, scarf.* PENINNAH *starts cutting food on her plate.*) No you won't. I'll back the car out. You'll scratch the side of the house. (*To* PENINNAH.) Peninnah, how about doing a little more eating and a little less playing with your food. Not that way! (*To* MITTY.) Walter, I wish you'd talk to your daughter about her table manners! (*Exits* L.)

MITTY. (*With authority.*) Peninnah (Pen-EYE-nah)—

PENINNAH. Peninnah (Pen-EE-nah)!

MITTY. (*Amused.*) Peninnah (Pen-EE-nah). (*Kisses her on cheek.*) Do you know one of the things that originally separated civilized man from the savage? (*She holds up knife and fork,* MITTY *nods.*) That's right! (*Takes knife and fork from her and proceeds to demonstrate.*) Here, let me show you how to do it.

MUSIC UP #3A

PENINNAH. Gee, Daddy, you do it so neat.

LIGHTS FADE

ACT ONE

SCENE 5

LIGHTS up on Surgical Dream. MACMILLAN *is wheeled in on operating room cart by* NURSES *and* DOCTORS.

DRIP, DROP, TAPOCKETA   *MUSIC CUE #4*

HEAD NURSE.	DOCTORS.
	Drip, drop, Tapocketa
	Drip, drop, Tapocketa
It's the billionaire banker	Drip, drop, Tapocketa
Wellington MacMillan	Drip, drop, Tapocketa
ALL NURSES.	
Wellington MacMillan	Drip, drop, Tapocketa
Billionaire banker	Drip, drop, Tapocketa
HEAD NURSE.	
Shhhhhh	Drip
ALL NURSES.	
Shhhhhh	Shhhhhh
DR. MITTY. (*Spoken in tempo.*) Who has the case?	Drip, drop, Tapocketa
HEAD NURSE.	
Doctors Renshaw, Benbow and Professor Remington	Drip, drop, Tapocketa
	Drip, drop, Tapocketa

ALL NURSES.

Lecherous Remington	Drip, drop, Tapocketa
Renshaw and Benbow	Drip, drop, Tapocketa

HEAD NURSE. (*Spoken in tempo.*) And Doctor Pritchard Dash Mitford   Drip

DR. MITTY. (*Shaking his head.*) Howja do!

(PRITCHARD-MITFORD *slaps his sword-like knife into* MITTY'S *hand, cutting it.* MITTY *reacts.*)

ALL NURSES.	ALL DOCTORS.
All the way from London,	All the way from London,
All the way from London,	All the way from London,
Doctor Pritchard dash	Yeh, yeh, yeh, yeh,
Mitford dash	Yeh, yeh, yeh, yeh,
All the way, all the way,	All the way, all the way,
All the way, all the way,	All the way, all the way,
All the way over from London!	All the way over from London!

(*Clap hand.*) London!	(*Clap hand.*) London!
(*Clap hand.*) London!	(*Clap hand.*) London!

HEAD NURSE.
Shhhhhh
MACMILLAN.
London!
ALL NURSES.

Shhhhhh	Shhhhhh
	Drip, drop, Tapocketa

DR. PRITCHARD-MITFORD.

(*Spoken in tempo.*) We've had	Drip, drop, Tapocketa
the Devil's own time	Drip, drop, Tapocketa
Obstreosis of the ductal	Drip, drop, Tapocketa

ALL NURSES. (*Spoken in tempo.*) Obstreosis of the ductal   Drip, drop, Tapocketa

DR. PRITCHARD-MITFORD.
(*Spoken in tempo.*) Tertiary
ALL NURSES. (*Spoken in tempo.*) Very, very, tertiary   Drip, drop, Tapocketa
Tertiary quite contrary   Drip, drop, Tapocketa

DR. PRITCHARD-MITFORD.   ALL DOCTORS.
(*Spoken in tempo.*)

Read your book, brilliant	Drip, drop, Tapocketa
Brilliant, wish you'd take a look	Drip, drop, Tapocketa

Mitty	Drip
DR. MITTY. (*Spoken in tempo.*) Glad to!	
ALL NURSES.	
Mitty said he's glad to,	Mitty said he's glad to
Mitty said he's glad to	Mitty said he's glad to
NURSE No. 1.	DOCTORS AND NURSES.
Oh my	
Gad we're glad, he said glad,	Yeh, yeh, yeh, yeh
ALL NURSES.	ALL DOCTORS.
Glad that he said that he's	Glad that he said that he's
Glad that he said that he's	Glad that he said that he's
Glad that he said that he's	Glad to (*Clap hand.*) Glad to
(*Clap hand.*) Glad to	(*Clap hand.*) Glad to
HEAD NURSE.	
Shhhhhh	
DR. MITTY. (*Spoken ad-lib.*)	
Glad to.	
ALL NURSES.	
Shhhhhh	Drip, drop, Tapocketa
	Drip, drop, Tapocketa
	Drip, drop, Tapocketa
	Drip, Tapocketa,
	Drip, Tapocketa,
HEAD NURSE.	Drip, Tapocketa,
	Drip, Tapocketa,
The	Drip, Tapocketa,
Anaesthetizer's	Drip, Tapocketa,
Giving away	
ALL NURSES.	Drip, Tapocketa,
Giving away	
HEAD NURSE.	Drip, Tapocketa,
Giving away	
ALL NURSES AND TWO DOCTORS.	TWO DOCTORS.
Giving away	Drip, Tapocketa,
ALL NURSES.	ALL DOCTORS.
Giving away—ah!	Giving away—ah!
DR. PRITCHARD-MITFORD. (*Spoken.*) And no one in the East knows how to fix it!	Tapocketa drip
ALL NURSES.	ALL DOCTORS.
The patient's slipping	Tapocketa, drip
The patient's slipping	Tapocketa, drip
He's slipping	Tapocketa, drip
Slipping	Tapocketa, drip

Slipping	Drip
Slipping	Drip
	DOCTORS AND NURSES.
	Drip, slip
	Drip, slip
DR. MITTY. (*Spoken.*)	Drip, slip
Quick	Drip, slip
My fountain pen	Drip, slip
Inside	Drip, slip
Coat Pocket	Drip, slip
There, that'll hold	Drip, slip
For ten minutes—	Drip, slip
Let's get on with it!	Drip, slip
	Drip, slip
	REMAINING DOCTORS AND NURSES.
Knife!	Drip, slip
	REMAINING DOCTORS AND
FOUR VOICES. (*Individually.*)	NURSES.
Knife, knife, knife, knife	Drip, slip
Knife, knife, knife, knife	Drip, slip
DR. MITTY. (*Spoken.*)	
Spatula!	Drip, slip
FOUR VOICES. (*Individually.*)	
Spatula, spatula, spatula	Drip, slip
Spatula	
Spatula, spatula, spatula	Drip, slip
Spatula	
DR. MITTY. (*Spoken.*) Egg-	Drip, slip
beater!	
FOUR VOICES. (*Individually.*)	
Eggbeater, eggbeater,	Drip, slip
Eggbeater, eggbeater,	
Eggbeater, eggbeater,	Drip, slip
Eggbeater, eggbeater	
DR. MITTY. (*Spoken.*)	
Thread!	Drip, slip
FOUR VOICES. (*Individually.*)	
T, H, R, E,	Drip, slip
A, D, NICE, RED	Drip, slip
DR. MITTY. (*Spoken.*)	DOCTORS AND NURSES.
Thread	Drip, slip
	Drip, slip
	Drip, slip
And, sew! . . .	

ALL NURSES.	ALL DOCTORS.
	Drip, drop, Tapocketa
	Drip, drop, Tapocketa
Hurrah, Halleluyah	Drip, drop, Tapocketa
Hurrah, Halleluyah	Drip, drop, Tapocketa
Doctor	Drip, drop, Tapocketa
Mitty	Drip, drop, Tapocketa
Hurrah, Halleluyah	Drip, drop, Tapocketa
Hurrah, Hallelu!	Drip, drop, Tapock!

BLACKOUT

ACT ONE

SCENE 6

LIGHTS up on Mitty kitchen, immediately thereafter. MITTY *and* PENINNAH *at table* L. *as before.* AGNES *enters* L., *crosses to table.*

AGNES. (*Puzzled.*) Walter, do you realize you've cut the ham into little pieces and put it all back together again?

MITTY. (*Dreamy.*) Huh?

AGNES. I will never understand you. And look at your tie!

MITTY. Huh? What's wrong with my tie?

AGNES. It's stained. Can't you see? It's stained. (MITTY *spits on tie, tries to rub off stain.*) And that's the tie I got you for our last anniversary. (*To* PENINNAH.) Peninnah, go upstairs and get your Daddy another tie.

PENINNAH. (*Crosses to stairs.*) What color, Daddy?

MITTY. Whatever color you like, dear. (*She exits* U. R.)

AGNES. (*Follows to be sure* PENINNAH *is out.*) Walter—

MITTY. Yes, Agnes?

AGNES. Walter, I'm worried about you. Have you been feeling all right lately?

MITTY. I feel great.

AGNES. You didn't sleep at all well, Walter.

MITTY. Didn't I?

AGNES. You mumbled in your sleep again.

MITTY. Did I?

AGNES. And when I came in just now you stared at me as if I were a complete stranger in a crowd. (*Sits. After a beat.*) Walter, who—who is Patricia?

MITTY. (*Puzzled.*) Patricia?

AGNES. Don't try to hide it, Walter. You talked about her in your sleep all last night.

MITTY. (*Chuckles.*) Oh, that's Patricia Nixon! You know, Pat!

AGNES. Why in the world would you dream of Pat Nixon?

MITTY. Well, she *is* the President's wife.

AGNES. Walter, I am worried about you. Lately you seem overly tense, nervous, irritable.

MITTY. Why do you keep saying that?

AGNES. Because lately you seem overly tense, nervous and irritable! ·

MITTY. You sound like an advertisement for something.

AGNES. You've been doing nothing but mumbling about women in your sleep. How do you explain that? First it was Madam Curie. (MITTY *gets a look in his eye.*) Then Josephine Bonaparte. (*A smile breaks across his face.*) And last week you checked into a hotel with Mary Todd Lincoln!

MITTY. Well, at least I keep company with a fine class of people, Agnes. (*Chuckles.*)

AGNES. This is a serious matter, Walter. (*Crosses to stairway R.*)

MITTY. Well, they seem like perfectly harmless dreams.

AGNES. I'm not so sure.

MITTY. Agnes, I wouldn't worry if I were you.

AGNES. (*Gazes upstairs.*) I have to for Peninnah's sake. Because if I ever thought you were— (*Turns on* MITTY, *shouting.*) Are you happy with me, Walter?

MITTY. (*Almost drops coffee cup.*) Agnes, for goodness sake, you nearly scared me to death! Of course I am. What kind of a question is that?

AGNES. Well, to tell you the truth, Walter, I'm of a good mind to send you to see Dr. Renshaw.

MITTY. Dr. Renshaw! You're kidding. He's a child phychiatrist!

AGNES. Yes, I know, Walter.

MITTY. That's ridiculous! I never felt better in my life.

AGNES. How can you, of all people, be so positive? Didn't you once say that the Vietnam War would last only two weeks?

MITTY. Well, you win a few, you lose a few.

PENINNAH. (*Enters* U. R., *gives tie to* MITTY.) Here, Daddy. Maroon.

MITTY. Thank you, dear.

AGNES. All right, Peninnah, get your things on and let's go. (PENINNAH *exits* L. *To* MITTY, *with machine gun rapidity.*) By the way, Walter, did you remember to make the payment on the mortgage? And when are you going to clean the cellar? And did you speak to the vet about the dog's ears? And have you decided where you're going to pick me up?

MITTY. Yes . . . Tomorrow . . . Not yet . . . And what was that last question . . . ?

AGNES. Walter, for a man who's forty years old today— (*Catches herself.*)

MITTY. What? What did you say, Agnes?

AGNES. (*Apologetically.*) I didn't mean to tell you. It slipped.

MITTY. (*Stunned.*) Today's my birthday?

AGNES. Peninnah and I were going to surprise you at dinner tonight. I'm sorry I—

MITTY. Agnes, you must be kidding? Forty years old—today?

AGNES. Yes. And honestly, for a man your age you certainly are acting like a child! (*Exits L.*)

MITTY. (*Total disbelief.*) But it can't be my birthday. How did it get here so soon? I'm not sure I'm ready to be forty years old. I'm not prepared yet! Where did all the years go?

MUSIC UP #5

MITTY. (*Takes off stained tie and looks at it.*) And what's happened to us, Agnes? (*Puts on new tie, jacket, etc. as he sings.*)

AGGIE

MITTY.
  Once I made you dream, Aggie, Aggie, Aggie
  Now I make you scream!

AGNES. (*Spoken Offstage.*) Walter!

MITTY.
  Oh Aggie what happened?

  Once I was your prince, Aggie, Aggie, Aggie
  Now I make you wince!

AGNES. (*Spoken Offstage.*) Walter, I'm waiting!

MITTY.
  Oh Aggie what happened?

  When it rained we waited for the rainbow
  When it stormed we laughed we joked,
  But now when it rains, what happens?
  Oh Aggie we get soaked!

  Once you were my life, Aggie, Aggie, Aggie,
  Now you're just my wife!

AGNES. (*Spoken Offstage.*) Walter, what's keeping you?

MITTY.
  Oh Aggie, what happened?

  Who's at fault?
  Now it's "Walter" and "Agnes"
  But once it was "Aggie" and "Walt."

*MUSIC SEGUES INTO #5A, AND THEN INTO #6. SEGUES
INTO CAR L. IN FRONT OF CLOSED SCRIM.*

LIGHTS FADE

ACT ONE

SCENE 7

*LIGHTS up on Mitty car, about ten minutes later. Throughout
scene,* AGNES *wipes imaginary window with Kleenex, re-
arranges imaginary rear view mirror, etc., while* MITTY
"drives." PENINNAH *sits in back seat.*

DON'T FORGET

AGNES. (*Sings.*)
Don't forget to get galoshes
down at Tom McAn, don't
forget you're meeting me, remember that's the plan, don't
forget to forget that little trip
to Harry's bar, if I told you
once I told you . . . Walter!
Watch that car!
   (*Talks.*)
Don't worry? The way you
drive, Walter! Peninnah, put
your collar up. Walter, close
that window before Peninnah
catches cold!

PENINNAH. (*Talks.*) Watch
out for the bumps, Daddy.
AGNES. (*Sings.*)
Don't forget to wear your
gloves, you know how cold
you get, don't forget to pick
up fertilizer from Korvette,
when you see Dr. Renshaw, tell
him all of your mistakes, if I
told you once, I told you . . .
Walter, quick the brakes!

WALTER.

(*Sings.*)
I saw him, I saw him
Don't worry, I saw him!

Forty, forty
I can't believe I'm forty.

(*Sings.*)
I saw him, I saw him
What's his hurry, I saw him

AGNES. (*Talks.*) You saw him! It's a lucky thing I screamed.
You act like you just got back from Harry's bar.

MITTY. (*Talks.*) Oh, Agnes, I only go there once in a while to watch a ball game and have a beer and chat with Harry . . . a man needs that kind of thing every now and then.

AGNES. (*Talks.*) A man doesn't. You do, Walter.

| AGNES. Keep to the right, Walter, do you want to kill us! And, of course you would have to lose that list, on purpose, I'm sure! Well, whatever you do . . . (*Sings.*) Don't forget, return that hat, you need it like the plague, don't forget, now none of that, you're starting to look vague! I'll just bet you weren't list'ning to a single word I've said! If I told you once, I told you . . . Walter! That light's red! You're driving like a clown, Walter, slow down! We're lucky we're alive, let me drive, Walter! | WALTER. (*Sings.*) Forty, forty, I can't believe I'm forty. Forty, forty, I can't believe I'm forty. I saw it, I saw it, I'm not dreaming, I saw it! Forty, forty, I can't believe it, no, I really can't believe it! |

MUSIC SEGUES INTO #6A, 6A FADES ON DIALOGUE.

BLACKOUT

ACT ONE

SCENE 8

LIGHTS up on Harry's Bar, later that afternoon.

HARRY. (*Behind bar.*) Let me get you a fresh beer, Walt. This one's on me.

MITTY. (*Sulking.*) Wha —? Oh sure, Harry. Thanks.

HARRY. You're certainly not acting like it's your birthday. What's the matter? Come on, tell old Harry.

MITTY. I'm just taking stock, Harry. Do you realize I've been spinning, spinning, spinning for 40 years and I've never woven a thing!

HARRY. So what do you want to do—start a back-to-the-womb movement? Hey, that might not be such a bad idea. At least you'd be guaranteed three square meals a day and central heating. (*No reaction from* MITTY.) Well, why not? It's very "in" to start movements today. Think about it, Walt. (*Shrugs.* MITTY *crosses to phone.*) Where ya going, pal?

MITTY. To call Agnes at the beauty parlor. What else? (*Inserts coin, dials.*)

HARRY. It's when I see you, Walt, that I go home and bless my bachelor heaven. (WILLA *and* IRVING *enter* U. L.)

WILLA. Hi, Harry.

HARRY. Hi, Willa.

WILLA. (*Crosses to bar.*) We just stopped off for a drink.

IRVING. Ah, Willa, you've had enough.

WILLA. Cool it, Irving. I want another drink.

IRVING. It's no good for you, Willa, putting all that junk—

WILLA. It's better than being addicted to that yummy yogurt of yours. (HARRY *hands her a drink.*)

IRVING. But the yummy yogurt comes in all different flavors!

WILLA. I know, Irving, but I always get hung up between cherry and pineapple. (*Holds up glass.*) See, vodka comes in one flavor. No decisions.

IRVING. Yeah, but yogurt's healthy for you.

WILLA. So is cod liver oil. So what?

IRVING. A little cod liver oil wouldn't hurt you.

WILLA. Hurt me—it would kill me! Oh, Irving, what's clean living ever done for you? By the time you finish doing push-ups, working out in the gym, eating all that imitation chopped liver and taking your steambaths—you're exhausted!

IRVING. (*Flexing his muscles.*) My body happens to be in terrific shape.

WILLA. (*Not impressed.*) I once knew a guy dead for three days—he had more energy than you!

IRVING. (*Indicates his muscles.*) Well, this is all muscle. (*Points to her drink.*) Alcohol will make you fat!

WILLA. Everything does, Irving. I only weighed four and a half pounds when I was born!

IRVING. You did? How did you keep alive?

WILLA. I sold newspapers.

IRVING. Come on, let's get out of here. (*Looks at watch.*) We're late for the bowling alley. (*Exits* U. L.)

WILLA. (*Gulps drink.*) One catastrophe after another. (*Crosses* U. L.)

HARRY. Go ahead, Willa. A little ride in a car might cheer things up.

WILLA. No such luck. Irving things cars are unhealthy. We've got a motorcycle outside. (*Exits* U. L. *as* RUTHIE *enters* U. R.)

RUTHIE. Are you Harry?

HARRY. Only if you're not a bill collector. What can I do for you?

RUTHIE. I'm Ruthie. Did a Fred Gorman call while I was in the ladies laboratory?

HARRY. Yup. On his way over, he said.

RUTHIE. Son of a bitch! Drags me here all the way from Toledo, then loses me. What's so special about Waterbury?

HARRY. What's so special about Mr. Gorman?

RUTHIE. Nothin'. Big talkin' fink big talks me into makin' a business trip with him an' all I'm gettin' out of it is old Claudette Colbert movies on TV and readin' the Gideon Bible. I even read the life story of Conrad Hilton three times!

HARRY. How about a little libation, Ruthie? You sound like you can use it.

RUTHIE. It's too early— (*On second thought.*) Well, make it something light.

HARRY. You name it.

RUTHIE. Double dry martini. (*Crosses to table* L.) I'll be at the table. Looks cheap, a girl alone at a bar. Son of a bitch! (*Sits.*)

MITTY. (*Into phone.*) Okay, Agnes. 'Bye, Agnes. (*Hangs up, crosses back to bar as* WILLA *enters* U. L. *She is disarranged and furious.*)

HARRY. (*Serving* RUTHIE *drink.*) Willa! What happened?

WILLA. I fell off the goddamn cycle—look at my knees, will you! (*Sits next to* MITTY.) Give me a drink before I lose my temper and open his skull with a barbell. Oh, and I got a gig in Hartford tomorrow. (*Dips Kleenex into drink and applies it to knee.*) I'll have to put pancake over them!

MITTY. (*Looking at her knee.*) Pancakes? Why don't you try mercurochrome? It's antiseptic.

WILLA. (*To* HARRY.) Another Irving! (*To* MITTY, *impatiently.*) Look, Tiger, I gotta sing. How can I sing with my knees scratched?

MITTY. (*Puzzled.*) How can you sing with your knees scratched? (*Shrugs.*) I really don't know.

HARRY. Where's Irving?

WILLA. Who knows? He loves that motorcycle so much—he never even looked back.

HARRY. Well, don't worry about it, Willa. Everything always works out for the best.

WILLA. (*Hotly.*) Who the hell ever said that?

HARRY. I think it was George Bernard Shaw.

WILLA. He had his nerve. I once saw a picture of Mrs. Shaw.

HARRY. (*Shrugs.*) Well, maybe it was Shakespeare. Between the two of them, they said everything! (MITTY *and* WILLA *sulk.*) C'mon you two, smile—you're on Hollywood Squares! In a minute you'll have them calling this joint Chez Miserables. (*No reaction.*

A thought.) Hey, see if this helps, I just heard it: A pregnant lady almost gets hit by a taxi while crossing the street. So the cab driver looks out and yells, "Hey, lady, you can get knocked *down*, too!" Get it—pregnant lady—knocked *down* . . .

MITTY. (*Delayed reaction.*) Oh, Harry, that's funny! (*Laughs. WILLA manages a faint chuckle, but is obviously more amused by MITTY.*) That's very funny!

WILLA. (*Turns to MITTY.*) Excuse me.

MITTY. (*Taken aback.*) Why, what did I do?

WILLA. My name's Willa.

MITTY. (*Relieved.*) Oh. Walter J. Mitty.

WILLA. Mitty?

MITTY. It rhymes with witty. (*She laughs warmly.*) No, it really does rhyme with witty.

HARRY. He's O.K., Willa. An old pal. Lonely, married, and a year older today.

WILLA. Well, in that case, you have a drink on me. (*Handing glass to HARRY for a refill.*) I wanna get smashed. (*To MITTY.*) My name's Willa de Wisp.

MITTY. (*A beat.*) That doesn't rhyme with anything.

WILLA. That's my stage name.

MITTY. Oh.

WILLA. (*Toasts.*) Well, here's to—

MITTY. To what?

WILLA. To the single life!

MUSIC UP #7

HARRY. Swear me in. There ought to be a law saying that marriage licenses should only be granted with old-age pensions.

MITTY. But I'm married! (*To WILLA.*) Aren't you?

WILLA. Who, me? No way.

MARRIAGE IS FOR OLD FOLKS

WILLA.
    When my kisses all misfire, I'll get ready to retire,
    When my best reflexes grow dull, I'll head for that wedded
        lull;
    This morbid bliss they rave about ain't for this miss, there
        ain't no doubt.
    I'll never give in while I'm young enough to give out!

    I love dancing, crazy romancing,
    Fellas advancing constantly,
    Marriage is for old folks, old folks,
    Not for me.

One husband, one wife, what d'ya got?
Two people sentenced for life!

I love singing, good healthy clinging,
Quietly bringing on a spree,
Marriage is for old folks, cold folks,
Not for me.

One married he, one married she, what d'ya got?
Two people watching T.V.!

I'm not ready to quit being free,
And I'm not willing to stop being me,
Gotta sing my song,
Why should I belong,
To some guy who says I'm wrong,
Ding a ding dong!

HARRY and MITTY.
  Ding a ding dong!

WILLA.
  Cooking dinner, looking no thinner,
  Red elbows, in a sudsy sea,
  Marriage is for old folks, old folks,
  But it's not for me.

  One husband, one wife, what d'ya got?
  Not my kind of life!

  I'm exploding with youth and with zest,
  Who needs corroding in some vulture's nest,
  Gotta fly my wings,
  Go places, do things,
  My freedom bell really rings,
  Ding a dong dings!

HARRY and MITTY.
  Ding a dong dings!
WILLA.
  I've been through years, too many blue years,
  Now I want New Year's every eve,
  Marriage is for old folks, old folks,
  That's what I believe.
    (*Sings ad lib.*)
  One bragging he, one sagging she. What d'ya got?
    (*In tempo.*)
  You sure ain't got me!

(MITTY *crosses to her carrying their drinks.* FRED GORMAN *and*
HAZEL *enter* U. L. GORMAN *spots* MITTY, *crosses to him.*)

GORMAN. Hey, Walter? Walter J. Mitty of Henderson Hall!
MITTY. Huh?
GORMAN. Long time no see!
MITTY. (*Surprised.*) For heaven's sake—Fred Gorman! (GOR-
MAN *embraces* MITTY, *almost crushing him.*)
GORMAN. Can you imagine meeting anyone in a town like this?
If they weren't rebuilding the sewer system you wouldn't find
Fred Gorman dead in this town! (*Notices* WILLA.) This looks like
the only live joint around. (*To* HAZEL.) Hey, baby, come over here
and meet somebody. (HAZEL *crosses to them.*) Walter J. Mitty,
the boy most likely to succeed—there it was in print!
HAZEL. (*With a heavy lisp.*) Succeed? In what?
GORMAN. (*Eyes glued on* WILLA.) You big lug, you. You
haven't changed a bit.
WILLA. (*Points to* MITTY.) He's over there!
HAZEL. I'm Hazel.
MITTY. (*Making introductions.*) Willa de Wisp—Fred Gorman.
And my friend Harry—he owns the place.
GORMAN. (*Reaches over instinctively and shakes hands with*
HARRY *without taking his eyes off* WILLA.) My pleasure.
HAZEL. I'm Hazel.
HARRY. Hiya. Any friend of Walt's—
MITTY. (*To* HAZEL.) We were roommates in college.
HAZEL. We were not! I didn't even know you! (*Crosses to bar.*)
GORMAN. (*To* WILLA.) Showbiz, I bet.
WILLA. You won your bet.
GORMAN. Willa 'n Walter—sounds like an old vaudeville team.
This is Miss Helen Clark—
HAZEL. Hazel. H-A-Z-
GORMAN. —an associate of mine.
HAZEL. Associate?
WILLA. She doesn't seem to recall the association.
RUTHIE. (*Furiously.*) Fred—over here—Ruthie!
GORMAN. (*To* MITTY, *under his breath.*) Oh, Jesus! Grab a
table, Walt—I'll join you in a minute. (MITTY *and others cross to
table* R. GORMAN *crosses* L. *to* RUTHIE.)
RUTHIE. I been waitin' for you for over an hour—
GORMAN. You gotta forgive me, baby. Big business. Important
contract.
RUTHIE. Who you kiddin'?
GORMAN. Now go easy, baby. That's Miss Helen Clark—she's
vice president of a big construction firm— (HARRY *helps* HAZEL
off with her coat. HAZEL *turns and gives a big smile to* GORMAN,

who half-heartedly smiles back.) Once I wrap up my deal with her, we're on our own!

RUTHIE. Yeah? Well gimme change for a *TV Guide* and I'll get the hell outta here!

GORMAN. (*Gives her a bill and a fast peck on the cheek.*) Here ya are, baby. I love ya. Goodbye. (*Crosses to table R.*) Get ready with the liquid fireworks, Harry, we're exploding tonight! And put it all on my tab.

RUTHIE. (*Storms over to* GORMAN.) You're a fink-liar, Fred. Her business ain't no bigger 'n mine! (*Exits U. L.*)

HARRY. Now, what's everybody drinking?

GORMAN. I'll have a martini on the rocks, extra dry, twist of lemon and no vermouth. Walter?

MITTY. (*Considers. The sophisticate.*) I'll have the same as Fred, Harry.

GORMAN. Willa?

WILLA. Make me a spare, Harry.

GORMAN. Helen'll have—

HAZEL. Brandy Alexander. And it's—

GORMAN. Brandy Alexander, Harry, and it's all on my tab. (HARRY *crosses to bar, mixes drinks.*)

MITTY. What are you doing in town, Fred?

GORMAN. Wheelin' and dealin'. Redevelopment contracts. Represent the third largest construction firm in the world. Travel everywhere.

WILLA. (*Removing his hand from under table.*) Well, watch where you're traveling now. My knees are scratched!

HAZEL. (*To* WILLA.) Excuse me, Miss de Wisp, but did you ever work at the—

GORMAN. (*To* MITTY.) Hey, Walt, guess who I bumped into just last week. Give you one hint. His name is Lester and he lives in Texas.

HAZEL. I knew a Lester from Texas. He—

GORMAN. (*Ignoring her.*) Lester Pfeffer!

MITTY. No! What's he doing?

GORMAN. Believe it or not, he's become the gum ball king.

HAZEL. (*To anyone who will listen.*) That's funny. I never heard of a—

GORMAN. (*Glares at her. To* MITTY.) Made a fortune selling gum ball machines. You know, married the ugly duckling daughter of the top brass. That's how some guys make it. Me, I made it on my own—no help. Four wives, too! (*To* WILLA.) Right now I'm on a sabbatical. (HARRY *serves drinks.*)

MITTY. You ever see Chuck Miller?

GORMAN. About a year ago. Lives down south. I don't

understand how a jackass like that got so lucky. Went into business with his old man the day he left college, and by spring carnival he was head of the firm.

HAZEL. I've never been south. The fartherest south I've ever been—

WILLA. (*Rises. To* HAZEL.) Honey, why don't you give up? (MITTY *also rises. To* GORMAN.) I hope we're not overcrowding you two. (*To* MITTY.) If you need me, Tiger, I'll be in the ladies room. (*Crosses* U. R.)

HAZEL. (*To* WILLA.) May I join you, Miss de Wisp?

WILLA. (*Imitating her lisp.*) Be my guest. (*Both exit* U. R. MITTY *sits.*)

GORMAN. Like they say, it takes two to tango. Never saw a man get up and say, "Hey, fella, will you join me in the john?" C'mon. Buddy Boy, own up—where did you hook that one? She's a cannibal!

MITTY. (*Amazed.*) You mean Willa? (*Hesitates, then confidentially.*) Oh, I got her out of my little black book, Fred. Under W.

GORMAN. I'll be damned! Are you still hitched, Walter?

MITTY. Yeah, sure. Twelve years now. But you just can't keep a man like me—

GORMAN. Don't I know it! We both suffer from the same bad habits.

MITTY. (*Significantly.*) Say, Fred, how do you like being divorced?

GORMAN. It's okay. At least I don't have to commute anymore.

MITTY. Must get pretty lonely for you, especially when you're on the road so much.

GORMAN. Lonely, hell! This country is lousy (*MUSIC UP #8.*) with three things, Buddy Boy—bars, banks and broads! And where the latter is concerned, Fred Gorman has his own system!

HELLO, I LOVE YOU, GOODBYE

GORMAN.
   When it comes to lovin' 'em and leavin' em,
   Dames can get outta hand.
   And when you're only in town one night,
   You only want a one-night stand!
      (*Spoken.*) Right!
HARRY. (*Spoken.*) Right!
GORMAN. (*Spoken.*) You know I'm right! (*Sings ad lib.*)
   Well I found a way to beat it!
   And here are the simple facts!

(*Sings in tempo.*)
When I make my play for a dame,
It's in three short acts!

Hello, I love you, goodbye!
That's my routine, I always break it clean.
Hello, I love you, goodbye!
Before the tears begin, I leave the scene.
We've had our moment of fun,
Well, that is that and so I grab my hat and say
I gotta run!
No fuss! No sir! No feathers, no fur to fly,
Just hello, little girl, I love you, little girl,
So long, little girl, goodbye!!
    (*Spoken.*) Come on, Walt, you try it with me!
MITTY. I really don't know whether I could—

GORMAN.	MITTY.
Hello	Hello
I love ya,	I love ya,
Goodbye	Goodbye
That's my routine,	
I always break it clean	
(*Talking.*) See what I mean?	
(*Singing in tempo.*)	HARRY.
Hello	Hello
I love ya	I love ya
Goodbye	Goodbye
Before the tears begin,	
I leave the scene,	

HARRY and MITTY. (*Talking.*) We see what you mean!

GORMAN, HARRY, MITTY.
    We've had our moment of fun,
    Well, that is that and so I grab my hat and say
    I gotta run!
GORMAN. (*Singing ad lib.*)
    No fuss! No sir! No feathers, no fur to fly,
GORMAN, HARRY, MITTY. (*Singing in tempo.*)
    Just hello little girl,
GORMAN.
    You're the cutest chick I've seen around
GORMAN, HARRY, MITTY.
    I love ya little girl,
GORMAN.
    Ya really lift my feet right offa the ground
GORMAN, HARRY, MITTY.
    Hello, little girl, I love ya little girl,

Don't cry little girl, goodbye!
(*Encore reprise.*)
GORMAN, HARRY, MITTY.
We've had our moment of fun,
Well, that is that and so I grab my hat and say
I gotta run!

No fuss! No sir! No feathers, no fur to fly,
Just hello, little girl,

You're the cutest chick I've seen around,

I love ya little girl,

Ya really lift my feet right offa the ground,

Hello, little girl, I love ya little girl,
Don't cry little girl, goodbye!

GORMAN. We'd make a helluva team, Buddy Boy.

MITTY. That's a good system, Fred. But, frankly, I've got my own system. (*Confidentially.*) Whenever I get the urge, I send the wife to her mother's and pull out the little black book. It's loaded.

GORMAN. Son of a gun. I should've gotten in touch with you sooner.

MITTY. Shame you didn't. I would've had them lined up for you—Buddy Boy.

GORMAN. Damn, that's what I really dig—a group scene! By the way, Walt, you know where I can pick up a little grass in this town?

MITTY. (*Without thinking.*) Down at the general store, I imagine— (*Catches himself.*) Oh, you mean *that* kind of grass!

GORMAN. You smoke once in a while, don't you?

MITTY. Once in a while? All the time, Fred, all the time! I even go to work every morning—stoned!

GORMAN. Good man!

MITTY. Don't worry, Fred, we'll get some later. And girls, too!

GORMAN. Now you're talkin'. Between you and me, know what the guys in the office call me? Wham-Bam-Gorman!

MITTY. Really? Know what the chaps at the yacht club call me?

GORMAN. Ut ut.

MITTY. Triple-Threat-Mitty!

MUSIC UP #9

(*TAPOCKETA THEME into Playboy Dream.*)

LIGHTS FADE

ACT ONE

SCENE 9

*LIGHTS up on Playboy Dream. The Mitty penthouse. The room
is empty.*

MITTY. (*Enters wearing smoking jacket and ascot. Lights up a
"joint" and takes a long drag.*) Ahhhh!

HARRY. (*Appears with notebook and pencil.*) Ready to order,
sir?

MITTY. (*After a thoughtful pause.*) I'm in the mood for bouilla-
baisse tonight, followed by coq au vin avec petits pois, and a
bottle of Bordeaux de Mitty Blanc, 1918.

HARRY. Brilliant choice, sir. And for dessert?

MITTY. I don't really know. What do you suggest?

HARRY. Any or all. They're yours for the taking, Monsieur.
(*Claps hands. Four exotic* GIRLS *enter* U. R.: *an alluring* FRENCH
GIRL, *a sexy, fiery* ITALIAN, *a trim, chic* AMERICAN COLLEGE GIRL
and a voluptuous, veiled TURKISH BELLY DANCER [AGNES]. *They
cross past* MITTY *for inspection as* HARRY *calls the name of each in
turn.*) Crêpe Suzette.

MITTY. Mmmmmm.

HARRY. Tortoni.

MITTY. Ciao! Ciao!

HARRY. Apple turnover.

MITTY. Like mother thought she used to make.

HARRY. Baklava.

MITTY. Baklava?

AGNES. Me Baklava.

MITTY. Baklava?

AGNES. Me Baklava.

MITTY. Mmmmm. (*Removes her veil.*) Baklava, hell! That's
Agnes! (*MUSIC OUT. To* HARRY.) Get her out of here!

AGNES. No, Walter. Me Baklava!

MITTY. Get her out of here!

AGNES. (HARRY *chases her around room.*) I can't bear it,
Walter. I'll kill myself!

MITTY. (*A little bored, a little annoyed.*) Agnes, don't make a
scene in my dream!

AGNES. (*At his feet.*) Don't throw me aside. Don't cast me into
the gutter to diminish into obscurity.

MITTY. Now please, Agnes. This is embarrassing.

AGNES. Without you, I'm nothing. You made me, Walter! Look,
I'm throwing myself at you—unashamed!

MITTY. (*To* HARRY.) Take her away! Please, Agnes. Out, out,

out! (HARRY *drags her off* U. R.) Isn't that pitiful! (*Then turns his attention to the* OTHERS.) You're all so luscious, I really don't know how to choose. All right—strip!

MUSIC UP #9 CONTINUED

(GIRLS *go into bump and grind strip routine.*)

STRIP

THREE GIRLS.

Take me, take me,
Don't you forsake me,
Don't make your Kitty bare and blue.
Mitty rhymes with witty,
Witty Mitty, and that's you!

GIRL No. 1.

You!

THREE GIRLS.

You!

GIRL No. 2.

You!

THREE GIRLS.

You!

GIRL No. 3.

You!

THREE GIRLS.

You!
Come on, enjoy me
Come on, destroy me,
What do we want,
To show you what we can do!
Hey there, 'Tiger,
Make me your mate,
Cause life without you's
One helluva fate!

AGNES. (*Enters* U. L., *begins to strip.*)

Oh Walter, don't leave me behind,
I'll do whatever I'm assigned,
No matter how hard the grind,
I'll do it and love it,
I'll do it and love it,
I'll do it and love it,
I'll do it and love it!

MITTY. Agnes, please! Get her out! (*MUSIC OUT.*) Get her out of here! (HARRY *carries her off* U. R. *on his shoulders.*) Isn't that pitiful? (*After a pause to catch his breath, he turns to* GIRLS *again.*) All right now, girls . . . let's take it off!

MUSIC UP AND FADE

BLACKOUT

ACT ONE

SCENE 10

LIGHTS quickly up on Harry's bar. GORMAN *and* MITTY *at* C. *as before.*

GORMAN. (*Gives him a big slap on the back.*) Whad'ya say to that, Triple-threat? Is that way-out or isn't it? (*Crosses* R. *and sits at table.*)

MITTY. (*Suddenly snaps to life.*) Huh? Oh, Fred! You shouldn't have done that then! Not just then! (*Shakes head. Crosses to table* R.)

GORMAN. Gonna have it put right in my will. I'll be the only guy ever buried in a Mercedes Benz! Can you picture that? When they lower me down, I'll be sitting right there behind the wheel—big as life!

MITTY. That's really living, Fred. (*Sits.*)

GORMAN. What about you, Walt? Ever make that million you were always talkin' about?

MITTY. I'm pretty close now.

GORMAN. What line are you in, Walt?

MITTY. Toys. The MacMillan Toy Company.

GORMAN. No kidding.

MITTY. We make toys.

GORMAN. No kidding!

MITTY. Confidentially, Fred, they're grooming me for the presidency. (WILLA *and* HAZEL *enter* U. R.) But frankly, I have some ideas of building a toy company of my own— (MITTY *rises as* GIRLS *approach.* GORMAN *remains seated.*)

WILLA. (*To* GORMAN.) On your feet, Prince Valiant. You're dealin' with ladies.

GORMAN. (*Rises.*) Sorry, ladies. (HAZEL *and* WILLA *sit.* MITTY *and* GORMAN *remain standing. To* GIRLS.) Buddy Boy and I were just talking over old times. We've come a long way since our old Henderson Hall days. (*Arm around* MITTY.) Tell 'em about the night, Walt, when the fellas took you down to Bella's house and chipped in to get you initiated, and you paid the girl ten bucks to leave you alone! (*Breaks into an infectious laugh.*) Tell 'em about that! Go on, tell 'em!

MITTY. (*Embarrassed.*) You just told them, Fred. (*They sit.*)

GORMAN. Well, times have certainly changed! Today any kid in first year high school would—

HARRY. (*At door* U. L., *yells.*) Willa! Irving just pulled up outside!

WILLA. Gimme "When the Saints Come Marching In" in the key of C. Irving is here.

MITTY. Who's Irving? (IRVING *enters, looks around, spots* WILLA, *crosses to* C.)

WILLA. Speak of the devil. (*Pretends to ignore him.*) Oh, Mr. Mitty, that's the funniest story I ever—

IRVING. Willa! Willa, you fell off!

WILLA. So did Lawrence of Arabia! Look, man, I'm busy now. I'm healing the wounds. Maybe there's a hot hopscotch game at the YMCA. Go play!

IRVING. I'm staying here.

HARRY. (*Crosses to him.*) Look, Willa's just having a nice, quiet drink with some friends— (IRVING *thrusts him aside, takes a ball out of his pocket, tosses it from hand to hand as he stands his ground.*)

WILLA. (*Loud enough for* IRVING *to hear.*) Excuse me while I deal with the big little boy. (*Crosses to bar with empty glass.*) Fill 'er up, Harry. (*Puts glass on bar.*)

IRVING. Ah, Willa, why can't you have tomato juice? It's only two o'clock.

WILLA. You're right. (*To* HARRY.) Bloody Mary!

IRVING. (*Crosses to table* L., *sits.*) It's going to be different when we get married, Willa.

WILLA. We ain't getting married, Irving—no way. Check out Jack La Lanne. He may be available! (*Sits.*)

IRVING. But I love *you*, Willa.

WILLA. Oh, jeez—can't ya see I'm depressed?

IRVING. I don't understand—what depresses you?

WILLA. (*Sharply.*) *You*, Irving.

IRVING. Any broad—I mean, any girl—would jump at the chance to get married and settle down.

WILLA. Then go find yourself a broad-jumper, Irving, and leave me alone. What I want you can't give me. (*To* HARRY.) I'll take it there, Harry. (*Crosses to bar, sits.*)

IRVING. (*Indicates room.*) Is this what you want, Willa? *This?* (*Crosses to bar, sits next to her.*) Tell me what you want in the whole wide world, and I'll give it to you!

WILLA. I only know what I don't want. I don't want to read any more of your poetry. I don't want to eat any more organic health foods. And I don't want to hear any more about that cabin in the hills of Ohio.

IRVING. Oregon!
WILLA. Oregon.

MUSIC UP #10

IRVING. (*Takes folded paper out of his pocket.*) Willa—
WILLA. Yeah?
IRVING. Look. "You're Oregon" by Irving Kornfeld.
WILLA. I'm what?

WILLA, WILLA

IRVING.

Willa, Willa, your pretty hair grows like the wild, wild rose,
Where the great trees rise and the sweet brook flows.

Willa, Willa, your smile is wide as the countryside,
Where the buttercup blooms and the butterfly goes.

Spring loves to sit on your shoulder,
And there's little bits of night in your eyes.

Oh, my Willa, Willa, while the great stars shine
And the green hills climb and the wild winds blow,

I will love you, Willa, I will love you, Willa,
I will love you so!

WILLA. (*After a thoughtful pause.*) Irving, I don't want night in my eyes. I want an opening night. And *I* want to be the great star that shines. On Broadway! Does that make sense? (*To* HARRY.) One opening night, Harry, in feathers and sequins—that's all I want—with lots of tall, graceful guys in tails! And I'll be doing my special material, "Fan the Flame" with lights—surprise pink and bastard amber!
IRVING. (*Embarrassed.*) Willa!
WILLA. (*Crosses to* IRVING.) After that, I'll be ready to go to Oregon, or pose with you for the cover of "Strength and Health" as Mr. and Mrs. Barbell. But first, I want my picture on the cover of *Time*. Pushups won't get me that, Irving. See?
IRVING. (*Nods "yes."*) No!
WILLA. (*Hands back his poem.*) Look, Irving, you're very sweet. But you're so damn healthy, you just make me sick! (*Crosses to table* R. IRVING *sits a moment, stunned, then crosses to her.*)
IRVING. Don't make fun of me in front of these people, Willa. And you ain't gonna make it!
WILLA. Wha—?

IRVING. You just ain't. I don't know much about show business—

WILLA. Well, you certainly don't!

IRVING. —but by the time you get there, you won't be healthy enough to sing—

WILLA. Look who's talking!

IRVING. —you'll be all choked up from the cigarette smoke, and exhausted from the late hours, and so nervous from drinking they'll have to carry you on!

WILLA. (*Fuming.*) You listen to me, Irving Kornfeld. I'll have you know I thrive on those things. Thrive on them, do you hear? I was born in—in the dressing room of a nightclub. So don't you tell me what's good for me and what ain't! (*Puts* MITTY's *arm around her shoulder.*) And these people happen to be my friends, so blow!

IRVING. Oh, yeah? (*To* MITTY.) Well, "friend," you just better take your hands off her!

HARRY. (*Crosses to* IRVING.) Look, Irving, why don't you be a good guy and— (IRVING *pushes him away.*)

MITTY. If she wants to be a star, she has a perfect right.

IRVING. I'm warning you, don't get any ideas! She ain't what she looks like!

WILLA. (*Stands.*) What? Ain't what I look like? (*Indignant.*) You get the hell out of here, Irving! I'm going to be a star. A big, fat, important star, do you hear me? And they're going to carry me through the streets. And I'm going to die tragically! And you're not going to have anything to do with it, Irving. Not a goddam thing! (*Sits, puts* MITTY's *arm around her again. Frightened,* MITTY *tries to get it back, but she holds on.*)

IRVING. (*To* MITTY.) Hey, what kind of ideas you been puttin' in her head? (IRVING *grabs and holds* MITTY *in his grip.* WILLA *screams as* GORMAN *and* HAZEL *rise.*)

GORMAN. (*Hands* HAZEL *a bill.*) Here, Helen, go pay the check. I'll get the car.

WILLA. (*To* IRVING.) If you don't cool it right now, man, our temporary separation will become permanent as of now!

IRVING. Willa, what separation?

MITTY. (*Desperately calls to* GORMAN.) Fred!

HAZEL. (*To* GORMAN.) Here's your change, Sweetie.

GORMAN. (*Gives it to* HARRY.) Keep it, Harry.

WILLA. Ours, Irving!

MITTY. (*Tries to reach out for* GORMAN.) Fred! Fred!

IRVING. I don't know what you're talking about, Willa!

WILLA. Let go of him, Irving!

GORMAN. (*To* HAZEL.) Come on, Helen, let's get out of here.

MITTY. (*Arms outstretched.*) Fred! Fred! (GORMAN *crosses* R., *shakes* MITTY'S *hand.*)

GORMAN. Good seeing you again, Buddy Boy. Take care. (*Exits* U. L. *fast.*)

MITTY. Fred! Buddy Boy! Hey!

IRVING. (*Releases him.*) Okay, okay. I ain't hangin' around here. (*To* MITTY.) But you and I are gonna meet on the outside, Old Man. Better watch out! (*Pushes* HAZEL *aside as he crosses* U. L. *and exits.*)

HAZEL. (*In doorway.*) Well, goodbye, everyone. It certainly has been unusual! (*Exits.*)

WILLA. (*After a pause.*) Thanks anyway, Tiger.

MITTY. For what?

WILLA. For coming to my defense.

MITTY. Defense? Are you kidding? I've never won a fight in my life!

HARRY. (*Very nervous.*) Okay, everybody, relax. He's gone. You get hurt, Walt?

MITTY. No, I'm fine. Just fine. Not a scratch.

HARRY. (*Angry.*) That big bully! Somebody ought to—

WILLA. Oh, never mind, Harry. Just give us another round. After all, we've got a birthday boy on our hands, remember?

HARRY. Yeah, sure. (*Crosses to bar.*) But if he comes back here—

MITTY. I don't feel much like a birthday boy.

WILLA. What are you talking about? Don't worry about Irving. He won't be back.

MITTY. Oh, it's not Irving.

WILLA. What then?

MITTY. Fred Gorman. I think seeing Fred kind of depressed me.

WILLA. Why?

MITTY. I wish I didn't have to see him today. Just not today!

WILLA. Are you kidding? You're a better man than Fred Gorman will ever be.

HARRY. You better believe it.

MITTY. You want to know something funny? In college I had to help him through math. Only now he doesn't have to count with his fingers anymore—he just snaps them and it's, "Yes sir." "What can I do for you, sir?" I'll bet he doesn't have to go in on Sundays for inventory either, or punch a clock, or sit in some stuffy cubicle. And when he dies, they'll probably put his name in *The New York Times.* And what have I done with my life? I went to bed one night full of dreams and ambitions—and woke up one morning forty years old with a wife, a child, a mortgage and a second-hand Chevrolet!

HARRY. Sounds like a helluva busy night to me!

WILLA. If that's the way you feel, then why don't you stop dreaming, Tiger. Be like me. Settle for the real thing or nothing.

HARRY. A man can do anything he wants to. Look at that famous artist who left his wife and everything to paint big, sexy, luscious women on an island somewhere. What the hell was his name?

WILLA. Xavier Cugat?

HARRY. No, not Xavier Cugat! Walt, listen to me. Supposing the doctor just told you you can't climb stairs any more—that you weren't long for this world—that your days were numbered. What would you do?

MITTY. Pray that he was wrong!

HARRY. But supposing he wasn't wrong? What would you do then?

MITTY. Stop praying.

HARRY. Then what?

MITTY. I'd cry.

HARRY. And then?

MITTY. I'd get hysterical!

HARRY. Now you're on the right track. Okay, okay, you have a year to live—like those people on *Medical Center*. What's the next thing you'd do?

WILLA. Say it, Tiger. Don't be afraid. (*To* HARRY.) That's his trouble, he's been too afraid all his life.

HARRY. You're telling me! Go ahead, Walt!

MITTY. (*After some hesitation.*) I'd—quit my job!

HARRY. Good!

MITTY. Sleep until noon!

WILLA. I'll drink to that.

MITTY. I'd shave only when I felt like it!

HARRY. What else?

MITTY. Burn all my neckties, wear sloppy clothes, go 'round and 'round the world, and never stop laughing!

WILLA. Now you're cooking!

HARRY. That's what I mean, Walt. You wanna spend some of your life sipping wine in a Paris cafe, don't you?

MITTY. Yeah, yeah!

HARRY. Dining on wienerschnitzel in Vienna?

MITTY. Yeah, yeah!

WILLA. And meeting the High Lama at the Taj Mahal?

MITTY. Definitely!

HARRY. Well? What are you waiting for?

MITTY. (*Back to earth now.*) It's impossible.

HARRY. I give up!

MITTY. (*Sorry for himself.*) Look, I'm the guy they arrest for walking on the grass.

WILLA. Only because you make yourself that guy, Tiger. You

can't just rest on your dreams, baby. You gotta work toward making some of them come true.

HARRY. I tell you, you can be as good as that swaggering oaf that just walked out of here! *You* can own a Mercedes.

MITTY. If I did, it would probably have a rattle in it nobody could find.

HARRY. And you can have as many ladies, too!

MITTY. Oh, women don't cry over me.

HARRY. (*To* WILLA.) Now he's unhappy because he's not an onion!

MITTY. Willa, do you think I've any sex appeal?

WILLA. (*Embraces him.*) Well, your cup doesn't runneth over, but you bring out the mother in me.

HARRY. I'm telling you, now's the time for action, Walt!

MITTY. The time? Oh, my God, what is the time?

HARRY. Four-thirty.

MITTY. (*Crosses to phone* L.) I was supposed to call Agnes an hour ago!

WILLA. Who's Agnes? (MITTY *inserts dime into phone.*)

HARRY. That's his legal guardian.

WILLA. (*Crosses to* MITTY, *takes phone out of his hand and hangs it up.*) Don't, Tiger. That's not where it's at.

MITTY. It's not?

WILLA. This is your one chance. I'm finished with Irving. You gotta be finished with Agnes. (*Starts to take him from phone. He turns, gets his dime back, then they cross to bar.*)

                                                              MUSIC UP #11

HARRY. Stand up to her like a man!

WILLA. It's time you tried.

HARRY. What can she possibly say?

MITTY. A few thousand choice words! (*Sits.*)

WILLA. We can try it together, Tiger, 'cause we're not looking for anything in each other.

HARRY. Walt, you got everything going for you. All you need now is one thing!

MITTY. What's that?

CONFIDENCE

HARRY.
Confidence!
Throw your shoulders back,
Confidence!
Be a whip and crack!   Stick your chin out,
                                        And you'll win out,
                                        Stand up, clear your throat
                                        Step out, strike a note of

Confidence!
Kiss your cares goodbye,
Confidence!
Blow your fears sky high,

You can do it,
There's nothin' to it,
Look up, touch a star,
Think big and you are!

Remember,
The world is full of people,
Plain old people like you,
Straighten up your tie,
Look 'em in the eye,
Believe what you say, and
they'll believe it too! Have
Confidence!
Give yourself the breaks,
Confidence!
You've got all it takes,

What's the difference
Between a zero and a hero,

Confidence!
Confidence!
Confidence!
That's all.
      HARRY and WILLA.
Confidence!
      WILLA.
Wear a see-through tie,
      HARRY and WILLA.
Confidence!

                    HARRY.
            Chase your rum with rye,
      WILLA.   Give your pills up
Tear your bills up
And hate Helen Hayes   Insult Willy Mays
      BOTH.
That's confidence!
      WILLA.
Sing your own duets,
      BOTH.
Confidence!

                    HARRY.
      WILLA.   Back my off-track bets, be
Increase your smoking,   provoking

Play golf on Mother's Day   Eat oysters in May,

Be carefree and lend your wife
your razor
Tho it's your very last blade,

BOTH.
Pat a porcupine, brush before
you dine,
Give up exercise
HARRY.
And don't deodorize,
BOTH.
That's confidence!
And it's all you need,
Confidence! brother, you'll
succeed,
What's the difference
Between
WILLA.
A nothin' and a somethin'
MITTY.
A dimple and a pimple!
HARRY and WILLA.
Confidence!
MITTY.
Confidence!
HARRY and WILLA.
Confidence
MITTY.
Confidence
HARRY, MITTY and WILLA.
Confidence, that's all!

HARRY.
A zero and a hero

SEGUE #11A UNDER DIALOGUE

MITTY. (*Crosses to phone.*) Harry, gimme a hundred dimes—
I'm gonna call them all . . . (HARRY *crosses to register, gets
dimes, then crosses to front of bar.*) I'm gonna turn in my insurance, and sell the house, then I'm gonna call MacMillan and
tell him to go to hell, and then I'll book passage for us, Willa!
(*Dials number.*)
    WILLA. (*Crosses to bar, sits on top of it.*) To everywhere and
anywhere . . . and I shall play there! No more dreamin' for you,
Pussycat . . . from now on it's Walter Mitty and Willa de Wisp
—live and in color!
    MITTY. (*Hangs up phone.*) The beauty parlor is busy, but when
I get Agnes, I'm gonna tell her to stay under the dryer until I pick
her up!

WILLA. When will that be?

MUSIC OUT. DRUM ROLL

HARRY and WILLA. (*After a pause.*) SAY IT!

MITTY. TEN YEARS FROM TONIGHT!

DRUM ROLL OUT. MUSIC UP #12

BLACKOUT

ACT ONE

SCENE 11

SPOTLIGHT immediately up on MITTY *at phone.* HARRY *and* WILLA *try to listen in.* HARRY *keeps feeding* MITTY *dimes throughout following number.*

TELEPHONE NUMBER

(NOTE: *In this number "Confidence, confidence" is always sung, but the rest of the lines are spoken rhythmically. Each "voice" appears in individual spotlight and represents various offices and homes in Waterbury.*)

ALL. (*Except* MITTY.)
Confidence, confidence

MITTY. Hello, is this the Met—

VOICE No. 1. You bet.

MITTY. —tropolitan Life?

VOICE No. 1. —tropolitan Life.

MITTY. Well, cash in Walter J. Mitty's insurance!

VOICE No. 1. You wouldn't!

MITTY. I would!

VOICE No. 1. You can't!

MITTY. I could!

VOICE No. 1. Wait'll I call his wife!

ALL. (*Except* MITTY.)
Confidence, confidence.

MITTY. Hello, is this the agent?

VOICE No. 2. Right.

MITTY. For Walter J. Mitty's house?

VOICE No. 2. Right.

MITTY. You're talking to Walter J. Mitty.

VOICE No. 2. Right.

MITTY. Have it sold by tonight!

VOICE No. 2. Right! Wait'll I call his spouse!

ALL. (*Except* MITTY.)
> Confidence, confidence.

VOICE NO. 3. Perry Travel Bureau . . . "Take a tip, take a trip, take two."

MITTY. Well, this is Walter Mitty and that's exactly what I'll do.

VOICE NO. 3. I've got two adjoining staterooms for a cozy tropical cruise.

MITTY. Sold!

VOICE NO. 3. Mister and Missus?

MITTY. Mister and Ms.

VOICE NO. 3. Hey, like wow, like hers and his. Wait'll I spread the news!

ALL. (*Except Mitty*.)
> Confidence, confidence.

MITTY. Is this MacMillan, MacMillan the villain?

VOICE NO. 4. This is the maid, the maid Adelaide.

MITTY. Walter Mitty speaking.

VOICE NO. 4. Oh—

MITTY. Is he in?

VOICE NO. 4. No.

MITTY.
> Well, just give him this message, see,
> Monday morning he's getting a letter,
> My letter of resignation, see.

VOICE NO. 4. Resig—what? Spell it please.

MITTY. Don't spell it, tell it, please!

ALL. (*Except* MITTY.)
> Confidence, confidence.

AGNES. (*In smock and curlers, with phone.*) Hello, Mother, you'll never guess what!

MOTHER. (*With phone.*) I guessed!

AGNES. You'll never guess who—

MOTHER. I guessed!

AGNES. It's Walter, my Walter!

MOTHER. Dead?

AGNES.
> I gotta go down to Harry's Bar
> Oh, Mother, the things they said!

(AGNES *removes smock and curlers, puts on hat and coat and exits angrily.*)

SEGUE TO #13

THE NEW WALTER MITTY

MITTY.
I'm gonna go quit my job, I'm givin' the ax to Agnes
Then I'm off to conquer the world
A trick that I can do cause I'm the new Walter Mitty,
The new Walter Mitty,
I made my mind up to wind up sittin' pretty,

WALTER.	GROUP.
Confidence	He's gonna go quit his job
Got my shoulders back	He's givin' the ax to Agnes
Confidence	Then he's off to conquer the world
I'm a whip, I crack	A trick that he can do cause
With my chin out	He's the new Walter Mitty
Why I can win out	The new Walter Mitty
I've got what it takes	He made his mind up
My foot's off the brakes	To wind up sittin' pretty,
Remember the world is full of people	Remember the world is full of people
Plain old people like me	*(Shouted.)*
	Like you

I'll straighten up my tie
Look em in the eye

Believe what I say	Believe what you say
And they'll believe it too!	And they'll believe it too

HARRY, MITTY *and* WILLA.

I'm (*He's*) gonna go quit my (*His*) job	Have confidence
I'm (*He's*) givin' the ax to Agnes	Give yourself the breaks
Then I'm (*He's*) off to conquer the world	Confidence

HARRY, MITTY and WILLA.

	GROUP.
A trick that I (*He*) can do cause	You've got all it takes
I'm (*He's*) the new Walter Mitty	What's the difference
The new Walter Mitty	Between a zero and a hero
With confidence	
	Confidence
Confidence	
	Confidence
Confidence, that's all!	Confidence, that's all!

CURTAIN

END OF ACT ONE

ACT TWO

SCENE 1

MUSIC ENTR'ACTE #14

LIGHTS up on Harry's Bar, early that same evening. HAZEL *and* RUTHIE *are at bar while* HARRY *keeps himself busy doing various chores.*

MUSIC FADES

RUTHIE. (*Toasts.*) To Fred Gorman—finkbubble!

HAZEL. May he smoke in bed! (*They sip drinks.*) I don't mind olives so long as they're pitless.

RUTHIE. Isn't that a coincidence? Me, too, Hazel!

HAZEL. God, I'm glad I met you, Ruthie.

RUTHIE. Must be a helluva feeling being stranded alone.

HAZEL. Did he tell you that if you got homesick he'd pay for—

RUTHIE. —for my mother to come in for a weekend? Yeah! He even told me—

HAZEL. —that his Uncle Ben is in wholesale furs! And I believed him. I feel like such a dope!

RUTHIE. It ain't that you're dopey, honey. It's that you're all heart.

HAZEL. Yeah, but at least other girls get stranded in Rome or Venice or someplace chic.

RUTHIE. I know what you mean. You don't feel like you got much class being stranded in Harry's Bar in Waterbury, Connecticut.

MUSIC UP #15

TWO LITTLE PUSSYCATS

RUTHIE.
  Meow.
HAZEL.
  Meow.
BOTH.
  Two little pussycats, that's our ilk,
  Wrestled with a restless dream,
  Of a land all satin and silk
  Where a pussycat bred on milk
  Could go crazy on cream!

50

Then one day, we met big Fred cat,
Looking for a place to prowl,
How we flipped when he tipped his hat
Smiled a smile like a welcome mat
And said, "Let's have us a howl"!
HAZEL.
He, monotonously, repeated his swell time bit,
RUTHIE.
And we, monotonously, repeatedly fell for it.
BOTH.
And now we're havin' a fit!
RUTHIE.
Meow.
HAZEL.
Meow.
BOTH.
Two little pussycats, as you've heard,
Having us a real good cry,
Oh how velvety smooth he purred
As we hurriedly got the word
"Hello, I love you, goodbye!"

Two little kittycats, drawn and drab,
Still we're learning the score,
When a tabbycat pays your tab
He won't settle for grateful gab
He wants a helluva lot more!

"There's a wonderful world right over that fence," he said.
"Just think, you'll wind up in mink,"
But, oh what a fink—instead
We only wound up in bed!
RUTHIE.
Meow.
HAZEL.
Meow.
BOTH.
We only wound up in bed!
HAZEL. (*Spoken.*) Pfzzt!
RUTHIE. (*Spoken.*) Sonofabitch!

SEGUE PLAYOFF #15A

(RUTHIE *and* HAZEL *exit* U. L. *just as* MITTY *and* WILLA *enter.*)

MITTY. Hey, Harry, we're back. (*An exchange of greetings.*) How about a little nectar of the gods?

HARRY. You got it. (*Crosses to bar.*)

MITTY. (*To* WILLA.) Dance, madam?

WILLA. Love to. (*Goes into a wild twist routine by herself.* MITTY *watches, amazed.*)

MITTY. Doesn't that hurt?

WILLA. It's fun. Try it.

MITTY. Not me. (*Then they dance slowly together.*) Ever been to a signature party?

WILLA. I've been to cocktail parties, pajama parties, acid parties, body-painting parties, and I even wound up at a wife swapping party once—but I must admit I've never been to a signature party.

MITTY. Well, you're going to one tonight! (*Half sings, half talks a few lines of "CONFIDENCE" as they continue to dance.*)

WILLA. Hey!

MITTY. What?

WILLA. You got all the papers?

MITTY. Does Rockefeller have money? (*Indicates pocket.*) Right here in my pocket, Willa. The insurance, the broker's listing, and my letter of resignation.

HARRY. (*Crosses with tray and glasses.*) Two martinis made with tender loving care.

MITTY. (*Waves* HARRY *away.*) No, no, Harry. That's for the tourists. We want a magnum of champagne!

HARRY. (*Stunned.*) Champagne?

MITTY. Okay with you, Willa?

WILLA. The only time I say no is when you ask me if I've had enough.

MITTY. May as well get used to it now. That's what we'll be drinking. Nothing but champagne!

WILLA. In bed.

MITTY. Of course.

WILLA. I can hardly wait.

HARRY. (*Shrugs.*) Okay by me. (*Snaps his fingers.*) Oh, Fred Gorman called back. Said he's all for joining us, and wants you to line up a blind date for him from your little black book.

MITTY. I'll show that Fred Gorman how to live, yet! ·

HARRY. (*Crosses to bar, turns.*) What little black book?

MITTY. Never mind, Harry. Never mind. (*Smiles mischievously.*)

HARRY. Oh, and in case you're interested, I've been spreading the word about the signature party. Got a whole bunch of people coming over.

MITTY. Good. Terrific, Harry. (HARRY *exits.* MITTY *and* WILLA *stop dancing.*)

MUSIC FADES

WILLA. Let's level, shall we, Walter J. Mitty—rhymes with witty?

MITTY. Okay.

WILLA. I always knew that someone, somewhere, was going to come along and straighten me out. But to tell you the truth, you weren't quite what I expected.

MITTY. I'm sorry.

WILLA. No, I'm glad it's you. Because you mean no strings. With you I can have my career without being chased around a room. I can take two weeks in Miami and come home with a golden tan instead of looking like alabaster. But most of all, I can share things with you, Tiger. You know something?

MITTY. No, what?

WILLA. I dig you.

MITTY. You do?

WILLA. (*Pokes him in gut with finger.*) Like fireworks in July.

MITTY. You're not lying to me, are you, Willa?

WILLA. I never lie. I mix up the truth once in a while, but I never lie! (*Kisses him tenderly. He over-anxiously tries to return the kiss, but she pulls away.*)

HARRY. (*Enters U. R. with magnum of champagne.*) I haven't opened a bottle of champagne since the building inspector was around for his payoff. Here we go . . . (*Cork pops. Expressions of delight as* HARRY *pours then gives each a glass.*)

WILLA. Thanks, Harry. (*To* MITTY.) Tiger—

MITTY. Yes, Willa?

WILLA. Do you think when we hit Paris I'll be able to get a job at the Folies Bergère?

MITTY. Sure you will. Of course you will.

WILLA. Can't you just see it? Me, with a lot of tall, graceful guys in white tails—

MITTY. (*The dreamer.*) Ah, were I one of those guys!

WILLA. —I can't wait! Won't it be wonderful, not having to enter through the kitchen any more! Marlene, make way— Willa is coming!

HARRY. I'll hoist one to that! (*They sip.*)

WILLA. (*An inspiration.*) Hey, I've got an idea. Before anybody comes, would you both like to see me do "Fan the Flame" right here? A special command performance!

MITTY. (*Excited.*) Sure, Willa. You bet we would.

HARRY. That'd be terrific.

WILLA. Of course, the costume I got now is kind of flakey. But my Folies one will be a knockout. You guys wait right here. (*Holds up purse.*) It'll take me just a minute to change. (*Exits* R.)

HARRY. (*Gives* MITTY *a friendly tap on the shoulder.*) You lucky son-of-a-gun.

MITTY. I know it. And I'll bet Willa sings pretty good. Oh, I can just see us now in Paris. (*Raises glass, toasts.*) Presenting that International Artiste, Mademoiselle Willa de Wisp and her great impresario—Sol J. Witty—rhymes with Mitty! (*Starts to look vague.*)

TAPOCKETA THEME #16
FAN THE FLAME (Part 1)
SEGUE TO #16

LIGHTS FADE

ACT TWO

SCENE 2

FAN THE FLAME (Part 2)

#16A (Instrumental solo and dialogue underscore.)

LIGHTS up on Folies de Mitty Dream. MITTY *is sitting at a ringside table.* CUSTOMERS *are drinking and talking at various other tables. In a moment,* GORMAN *enters* U. L., *crosses to* MITTY.

GORMAN. Ah, Walter, mon ami. I have been looking for you.
MITTY. Hello, Freddie. How are you?
GORMAN. You haven't forgotten my blind date from your *Petit Livre Noir?*
MITTY. Ah, Freddie, I would not let you down. She is right over there, waiting. (*Indicates* GIRL *at bar.*) Ex-Folies girl.
GORMAN. I am so happy I found you. Thank God.
MITTY. I shall.
GORMAN. I heard you were a friend of His! (*Crosses to* GIRL.) Hallo—je t'adore. (*To* MITTY.) Au revoir. (IRVING *enters* U. R. *carrying tray and champagne.*)
MITTY. (*To* IRVING.) Garçon! Champagne, s'il vous plaît. Ici! (IRVING *crosses and serves him, then starts crossing* R. MITTY *sips drink, spits it out. Angrily.*) Domestique! (*To* IRVING.) Garçon—voilà! (IRVING *crosses back.* MITTY *slaps his face with gloves.*)
IRVING. I don't think that's funny! (*Exits* U. L.)
MITTY. On with the Spectacular!

MUSIC OUT. DRUM ROLL.
HARRY. (*Enters* U. R. *With bad French accent.*) Attention,

Mesdames et Messieurs. Attention, world! Tonight we will not perform "The Red Shoes." Instead, we have the pleasure of presenting for the first time here in Paris—direct from Hartford, Connecticut, la magnifique, la fantastique, la tragique, Mademoiselle Willa de Wisp—in person!

DRUM ROLL. MUSIC UP INTO #16B

(HARRY *exits* U. L. BOYS *enter* U. R.)

FAN THE FLAME   *Part 3 (#16B.)*

BOYS.
    Who is Cupid's curvy dart?
    Whose lament tears you apart?
    Who can it be, hey who, who, who can it be?

    When she struts her torchy stuff,
    Mister, you can't get enough.
    Who can it be, hey who, who, who can it be?

    It's that . . . moment,
    Here she comes,
    Crash the cymbals,
    Beat the drums,
    It's that swell, ringading belle, Willa de Wisp
    Yessirree, direct from Hartford to Paree, Paree, Paree, oui,
    Oui!

    Now that we've told you,
    Get ready to cheer,
    You're gonna flip,
    Our little chanteuse is here,
    Willa de Wisp, crisp and how, Willa de Wisp,
    She's a wow
    Hey lovely lady take a bow, a bow, a bow, hi Willa!

(BOYS *are facing* R.)

DIRECT SEGUE TO #16C

FAN THE FLAME Part 4 (16C)

WILLA. (*Offstage.*)
    La La La La La La La
    La La La La La La La
        (*Enters* U. L. *Throws a kiss to* MITTY.)
    Fan the flame, feed the fire
    Fill my heart with a warm desire,

Hold me close, close like this
Let the magic ending be our two lips blending!

Light the coals, stir the embers
Give the love that a heart remembers
Sizzling hips, they're yours alone
Why this hesitation, start a conflagration!

Oh my precious lover, help me to discover
Just how high my eager heart can fly!
Come on and fan it, fan it, fan the flame,
Feed it, feed it, feed the fire,
Angel one, you're my one desire,

I've got a heart that I wouldn't mind losing
If love were the name of the game,
So let the passion smoulder, and tiger, please

La La La!

Oh my precious lover, help me to discover
Just how high my eager heart can fly,
Come on and fan it, fan it, fan the flame
Feed it, feed it, feed the furnace
You've got the torch
So come on, come on, come on and burn us.
    (*Monologue.*)

                MUSIC CONTINUES UNDER DIALOGUE
He has walked out of my life. It all started the day he lost his
accordion. He said I was to blame—and he beat me again—
After he walked away I ran through the streets crying, "Où est-il,
où est-il—mon heel, mon heel"? But no answer. Only the sound of
his accordion. What was I to do? Then all faces became his face—
and I gave myself to them. Because them was him. I became
known throughout Pigalle as Willa la Douce! Then one night I
learned that he was somewhere in Morocco fighting with the
French Foreign Legion and I stood in front of Notre Dame and
called . . . mon homme! (*Sings.*)
    Light up the wick of this simmering chick,
    And we'll fly to a fiery fame,
    I'm just a can of sterno, so
    La La La!
Boys.
    Fan the flame!
    Fan the flame!
    Fan the flame!

WILLA.
Fan it!
(WILLA, *surrounded by admirers and flowers, blows another kiss to* MITTY. *He toasts her. Applause.*)

BLACKOUT

ACT TWO

SCENE 3

LIGHTS up on Harry's Bar, as before. MITTY *is still at bar, in a slight trance, toasting an imaginary* WILLA *with his empty glass.* HARRY *watches for a moment, shakes his head, then clicks his fingers in front of* MITTY'S *face.*

HARRY. Walt? Hey, Sol!
MITTY. Huh?
HARRY. Abandon ship!
MITTY. (*Slowly snapping out of it.*) Oh, Harry? I was, er, just thinking about Paris.
HARRY. Is that what you were doing? I thought you were conducting a seance for one! (*Pouring champagne.*) Boy, I sure wish I was going with you.
MITTY. What's stopping you, man? You gotta have confidence! (*Winks.*) Say, Harry, did you know that Willa was literally born in a trunk?
HARRY. No kidding!
MITTY. That's right. Her mother—she was a singer, too, you know—
HARRY. No kidding!
MITTY. That's right. And she had just finished her act and they couldn't find a doctor, so Willa was delivered by the prop man!
HARRY. No kidding!
MITTY. That's right.
HARRY. Will you please stop saying "that's right!"
MITTY. Will you please stop staying "no kidding!"
HARRY. How do you know all that about Willa and her mother?
MITTY. Willa told me.
HARRY. (*Snaps fingers.*) Son-of-a-gun, I should've guessed.
MITTY. Willa's had a real rough life, poor kid. No money, no roots. Why, sometimes they didn't even have enough money for food, so Willa had to learn to steal at a very early age.
HARRY. Gee, I imagine it must be pretty tough stealing a well-balanced meal—so many proteins, so many carbohydrates—

MITTY. Yeah. But from now on, all that's going to be changed. For both of us. Why, I feel like a prisoner who's been locked up for twenty years and, suddenly, somebody's handed me a machine gun! What a sense of power I feel! I'm a new man. I tell you, Harry, I'm indestructible! (*PHONE rings.*)

HARRY. (*Handing* MITTY *bottle of champagne.*) Here, Indestructible, pour. I'll get the phone. (*Crosses to phone, answers it.*) Harry's Bar. Who? Willa? Er, just a minute, I'll see. (*Covers mouthpiece, calls Offstage.*) Willa. It's for you!

WILLA. (*Offstage.*) Who's calling—the creep?

HARRY. Sounds more like Neanderthal Man. Are you here?

WILLA. (*Offstage.*) Of course I'm here.

HARRY. What do you want me to tell him?

WILLA. (*Offstage.*) Tell him to hold his weights, I'll be right there.

HARRY. (*Into phone.*) Hold your— (*Catches himself.*) Er, hold on. She'll be right here.

WILLA. (*Enters in street clothes, as before. She crosses to phone. Apologetically, to* MITTY.) Sorry, Tiger. I'll do "Fan the Flame" for you right after I take care of Muscles. (*Grabs phone from* HARRY.) Give me that. Am I going to tell him a thing or two! (*Into phone.*) Hello—

LIGHTS FADE TO HALF

ACT TWO

SCENE 4

SPOTLIGHTS up on WILLA *at phone, and* IRVING *in Steamroom.*

IRVING. (*Into phone.*) Willa, this is Irving.

WILLA. Whaddya hear from your head?

IRVING. I called to tell you I got to the Y all right.

WILLA. That's a scoop for Associated Press.

IRVING. In case you were worried. I'm sorry about what happened this afternoon, Willa.

WILLA. Irving, it's a pleasure to hear you breathing hard. Where are you?

IRVING. In the sauna.

WILLA. Groovy. (*To* MITTY *and* HARRY.) Sauna! Are you ready?

IRVING. Excuse me, I got perspiration in my eyes. (*Puts phone on lap.*)

WILLA. Oh, my God! Irving? Irving?

IRVING. (*Puts phone to ear.*) Yeah, Willa?

WILLA. Irving, do me a favor.

IRVING. Anything you say.

WILLA. Wish me bon voyage and take a cold shower.

IRVING. Bon Voyage? Hey, that means you're going somewhere in French!

WILLA. That's right, man.

IRVING. How?

WILLA. For your information, I'm off to see the world.

IRVING. How?

WILLA. Irving, you sound like an Indian in heat!

IRVING. I'll follow you, Willa. I don't care. I'll find a way. What'll you do then?

WILLA. (*Laughs.*) Put you in the act. I'll buy you a gold bikini and you'll carry me down a big staircase over your head and it'll be the goddamdest entrance any girl ever made! (*He slams the phone down and exits.* WILLA *hangs up, turns to* MITTY *and* HARRY.) He's intensely disturbed!

SPOTLIGHTS OUT

ACT TWO

SCENE 5

LIGHTS up full on Harry's Bar.

MITTY. That's what Agnes says about me.

WILLA. You're not disturbed, Tiger. Just a little uptight.

MITTY. You want to hear something funny?

WILLA. Go!

MITTY. She thinks I ought to see a psychiatrist.

WILLA. (*Crosses to bar.*) I knew a girl who went to see one once. She freaked out when she found out the other girls she worked with were getting paid!

HARRY. Funny, Willa. Funny.

MITTY. (*Shaking his head.*) Can you imagine her suggesting that to me—a grown man!

HARRY. Well, who the hell would you expect to go? The newly born?

WILLA. How come your wife wants you to see one?

MITTY. Because I happened to dream about Pat Nixon last night.

WILLA. On second thought, maybe Agnes is right—you do need a shrink.

MITTY. I do not. (*Considers.*) Sometimes I think I hate that woman.

WILLA. Who—Pat Nixon?

MITTY. No. Agnes.

WILLA. Now that's silly. You shouldn't hate anybody. Despise them, yes. Hate, no.

HARRY. That's a pretty good philosophy, Willa.

MITTY. You know what?

WILLA and HARRY. What?

MITTY. I think Agnes is the one who needs the shrinker. (*As he begins to look vague:*)

MUSIC UP

(*TAPOCKETA THEME #17. Into Psychiatrist Dream. LIGHTS FADE.*)

ACT TWO

SCENE 6

LIGHTS up on Psychiatrist Dream. Hanging in the background is a banner proclaiming, "SUPPORT MENTAL HEALTH." Also visible are two Thurberesque drawings of DR. FREUD and DR. MITTY. Sitting D. S. in a semi-circle are the 4 or 5 PATIENTS. In a moment, MITTY enters U. C. and observes them as they babble incoherently to each other.

MITTY. Good morning, Group!

GROUP. Good morning, Doctor.

MITTY. (*As they continue babbling.*) I'd like you all to meet our new member. (*Indicates AGNES who sits in C. of semi-circle.*) Mrs. Walter J. Mitty. You see, Mrs. Mitty:

SHE'S TALKING OUT

MITTY.
They're talking out their problems
That's the very best thing to do,
Talk, talk, very best thing,
The very best thing to do.
GROUP.
We're talking out our problems,
That's the very best thing to do,
Talk, talk, very best thing,
The very best thing to do.

MITTY. (*Spoken.*) You see, Mrs. Mitty, how good, healthy talk is helping them. Now, forget your dementia-pretentia, and lift the lid on your id.

AGNES. (*Sings.*)
> Please believe me, dearest group,
> I've only one complaint;
> Do you know what life is like,
> When wedded to a saint,
>
> Not to mention millionaire
> Whose every deed the crowds applaud,
> The confidante of presidents
> And in fact a friend of Gawd?

MITTY.
> She's talking out her problem
> That's the very best thing to do
> Talk, talk, very best thing,
> The very best thing to do.

GROUP.
> She's talking out her problem
> That's the very best thing to do,
> Talk, talk, very best thing,
> The very best thing to do.

MUSIC CONTINUES UNDER DIALOGUE

MITTY. Now, I'd like a few of you to introduce yourselves to our new member.

JUVENILE DELINQUENT. (*Knitting.*) I got hit over the head during a non-violent demonstration. I couldn't remember who I was so came to Dr. Mitty's therapeutic sessions. He said if I started to knit, I might find out who I was. So I started and now I know who I am! (*Proudly holds up knitting, showing red, white and blue striped pattern.*) I'm Betsy Ross!

NYMPHOMANIAC. (*She sits dipping a comb into a large honey-colored jar and combing her hair.*) I was born in Scarsdale . . . slightly oversexed. So in no time at all I became bored with conventional libido drives. Let's face it—I'd had it!—and everybody! There was only one thing left to do and delicious Dr. Mitty recommended that. "Lock yourself in a room," he said, "and comb honey through your hair." God, he was so right!

MITTY. Now, Mrs. Mitty, talk, you poor, sick soul, talk.

AGNES. (*Sings.*)
> Just to fetch his slippers in
> Would burst my heart with pride
> Oh but something evil holds me back

Each time I've tried;
Tho' I yearn to heed his every need,
I only twit and twitch;
Dear group if you can help
I'll gladly give up every stitch;
I'll do it and love it,
I'll do it and love it,
I'll do it and love it!

MITTY.
She's talking out her problem
That's the very best thing to do,
Talk, talk, very best thing,
The very best thing to do.

GROUP.
She's talking out her problem
That's the very best thing to do,
Talk, talk, very best thing,
The very best thing to do.

MITTY. There, there, troubled woman. You desire to walk in the light of your husband's glory, but something evil does, indeed, keep you from it. Can the group suggest a cure?

GROUP. (*In unison.*) Painting! Telephoning! Sit on your hands! Aardvark! Knitting! Honey!

MITTY. Alas, no, dear group. Hypnosis!—with just a pinch of shock. (*Waving his hands at* AGNES *with typical hypnotic gestures.*) Tapocketa . . . tapocketa . . . tapocketa-pocketa . . . tapocketa! And now, Mrs. Mitty, when I clap my hands, you shall rid yourself of the evil that keeps you from serving your remarkable husband. (*Claps his hands as she yanks a book from her purse and holds it out to him.*) Aha! Just as I suspected! This month's *Reader's Digest.* (*Tears it to shreds.*)

GROUP. (*Sings.*)
Our brilliant Doctor Mitty
Knew the very best thing to do,
Talk, talk, very best thing,
The very best thing to do.

Yes brilliant Doctor Mitty
Knew the very best thing to do,
Talk, talk, very best thing,
The very best thing to do!

SEGUE TO SCENE CHANGE. MUSIC #17A

BLACKOUT

ACT TWO

SCENE 7

LIGHTS up on Harry's Bar, immediately thereafter. HARRY, WILLA *and* MITTY *at bar.* MITTY *sits tearing a napkin to shreds.*

MUSIC FADES ON DIALOGUE

WILLA. (*Poking him playfully.*) Hey, Tiger!

MITTY. Huh?

WILLA. Stop dreaming and talk to us.

MITTY. I wasn't—

WILLA. (*To* HARRY.) Hit me again, Harry. I don't want to lose my glow. (HARRY *pours another round of drinks as* TOWNS-PEOPLE *enter* U. L.)

PETE. Harry, we're all here! (*Ad lib greetings.*)

WILLA. (*To* MITTY.) Look, Tiger. Your party has arrived.

MITTY. That's great! (*To* GROUP.) You're just in time to help me celebrate! Hey, everybody, let's drink to the signing of my new declaration of independence. I've got all the papers right here—the broker's listing, the insurance, and my letter of resignation.

PETE. Where are you off to first?

WILLA. Paris! (*To* MITTY.) Right, Tiger?

MITTY. Right on!

HARRY. (*Throws a kiss to the air.*) Don't forget to give my regards to St. Germain!

MITTY. (*Toasts.*) C'mon, everybody, down the old rabbit's hole! To my New Year! (*Glasses clink.*)

MUSIC UP #18

NOW THAT I AM FORTY

WILLA. (*Standing; ad lib.*)
You'll grow a beard and you'll paint in Seville,

HARRY. (*Makes castanet sound.*)
You'll have sweet slender maids feed ya nuts in Brazil,

MITTY. (*Clicks heels.*)
I'll join the Swiss Ski Patrols
(*Does ski swish.*)

I'll search the Dead Sea for scrolls
(*Does searching bit.*)
I know I'm not dreaming, I really will

GROUP. (*In tempo.*)
You really will, of course you will,
You will, of course you really will!

MITTY.

Now that a I am forty, I'll win a Pulitzer
Two or three and that hot line from Russia to us sure
Will go through me!

GROUP.

Walter Mitty!

MITTY.

I'll play Santa Claus to the nation's poor on each
    Christmas Day,
Of course the New York Times will headline each
    precious word that I say!

TWO MEN.

Walter Mitty!

MITTY.

Rushing, off to Rio, in my private plane

HARRY and WILLA.

With your oil wells gushing, you'll do Paris

MITTY.

When I tire of Spain!

ONE MAN.

Olé!

(DANCE INTERLUDE.)

WILLA.

Now that you are forty, we'll breeze along in your Bentley
    coupe,
Oh boy, oh boy, won't I look sporty on board your forty-
    foot sloop!

GROUP.

Walter Mitty!

HARRY and WILLA.

Riding yaks in winter, down in Samarkand,

MITTY.

Picture me deciding to safari in Somaliland!
    (Dance interlude.)
I know I'm not dreaming, I really will.

GROUP.

You really will, of course you will
You will, of course you really will!

MITTY.

Now that I am forty, I'll be a millionaire once or twice,
Wall Street Bankers clamoring for my brilliant advice,

GROUP.

Walter Mitty:
Out at Yankee Stadium in your private box you'll relax.

While your accountants try to figure out how to lower your
   tax.
HARRY and WILLA.
   Walter Mitty!
MITTY.
   Ranching L.B.J. style, gee, that might be fun,
HARRY and WILLA.
   While your banks are branching,
   And your blue chips splitting two for one!
MITTY.
   Two for one?—Ten for one!
GROUP.
   By what genius touch you'll zoom right up to the top
   You don't know,
MITTY.
   But I know this much, that I'm getting there
   Now that I'm
GROUP.
   Now that you're
MITTY.
   Four-O!
GROUP.
   Walter Mitty, the greatest in the land, olé!

SEGUE TO PLAYOFF #18A

MITTY. (*Feeling no pain.*) Thank you, one and all, for helping
me celebrate this day. (*Ad lib to cover* TOWNSPEOPLE *sitting at
various tables. To* WILLA.) It's turned out to be the most wonderful day of my life!

HARRY. (*At door,* U. L., *shouting.*) Walt, Agnes just pulled up
outside! She's here!

MITTY. (*Stunned.*) Agnes—here?! If she finds me like this,
she'll—

AGNES. (*Offstage, rapping on door.*) Walter? I know you're in
there, Walter! Let me in or come out this minute!

HARRY. (*To* WILLA *as he puts his weight against door.*) You
better hide him quick or he's a dead duck!

AGNES. (*Offstage.*) All right, Walter, if that's the way you want
it! First thing Monday morning it's Dr. Renshaw for you—I'm
not fooling!

MITTY. (*To himself.*) No, not Dr. Renshaw. I won't go!

AGNES. (*Offstage.*) And I'm going to take you myself! (*Pounds
on door.*) Walter! Walter, what is this nonsense?

HARRY. (*To* MITTY.) Will you get lost!

AGNES. (*Offstage.*) Let me in this second or I'll call the police.

HARRY. (*To* MITTY.) Agnes is out there, Walt. Do you understand—Agnes!

AGNES. (*Offstage.*) Your last chance, Walter!

MITTY. I know, but what can I do?

HARRY. (*To* WILLA.) Willa, give him a hand, will you! Get him into the john—do something—quick! I can't hold the door forever.

WILLA. I've got an idea. (*Hands scarf and coat to* MITTY.) We'll smuggle you out! (MITTY *nervously crosses* D. R.) Hold it, Tiger—wrong john! Go into the ladies room. Wait, take my compact. You'll need some rouge to make it look authentic.

MITTY. Right.

HARRY. Hurry up! I think she's stronger than I am!

WILLA. (*Fumbles for compact, then hands* MITTY *her purse.*) Here, take it all!

AGNES. (*Offstage.*) I shall ask one more time—open this door!

HARRY. (*To* WILLA.) Willa, you take care of Agnes. I'll give Walt a hand. (WILLA *crosses* U. L. *as* MITTY *and* HARRY *exit* U. R. *Pause.* AGNES *enters, enraged.*)

AGNES. All right, where is he?

WILLA. (*Stops dead in her tracks.*) He? Who he?

AGNES. Has my husband been here?

WILLA. (*Cool.*) Haven't the foggiest, honey. Who's your husband?

AGNES. Walter Mitty. (*Takes a quick look around.*) What's going on? Why was the door locked? Who's in charge? Where's Harry? He owns this place, doesn't he?

WILLA. How does your husband manage to answer all those questions at once?

AGNES. He doesn't. That's the trouble. I have a feeling Harry's covering up something.

WILLA. I wouldn't know about that, honey. Harry and I are in different professions.

AGNES. Oh, if Walter only knew what he was doing to me.

WILLA. Why, hasn't he ever done it before?

AGNES. Only once. When we were first married. We had a terrible argument and he left the house to go to his club.

WILLA. What happened?

AGNES. Nothing. He forgot he didn't belong to any club!

WILLA. Oh, honey, you don't know when you're well off. I got one who's a member of everything but the human race. That's the battle of the sexes, I guess. How about a drink?

AGNES. What?

WILLA. (*Indicates her glass.*) Some booze.

AGNES. I don't drink, thank you.

WILLA. (*Mimicks her under breath.*) I don't drink, thank you.
(*Enter* FRED GORMAN *and* SYLVIA U. L.)
GORMAN. (*To* WILLA.) Well, here I am. I hope I didn't miss anything! Where's Walter? I want everyone to have a drink on me. It's a special occasion when a man gets up enough courage to leave his wife!
AGNES. He is here! I knew it!
GORMAN. (*To* AGNES.) Oh, you must be my blind date, huh? (*Shrugs.*) Well, I'm glad I brought along a spare. (*Snaps fingers.*) Sylvia!
SYLVIA. (*Crosses to* GORMAN.) I feel like some chop suey. Are we gonna eat?
GORMAN. I just fed you.
SYLVIA. So—can't I feel like some chop suey?
GORMAN. No. (RUTHIE *and* HAZEL *enter* U. L.)
RUTHIE. Harry, did I leave my purse here before?
HAZEL. (*Taps* RUTHIE *on shoulder.*) Say, Ruthie, never mind your purse. (*Indicates* GORMAN.) Look who's here, will ya—
RUTHIE. Yeah—and look at that *thing* he's hangin' on to. (*Shouts.*) Hey! Fred Finkbubble!
GORMAN. (*Looks up, surprised, slightly nervous.*) Hiya Ruthie. Hazel. Where you girls been? I've looked all over town for you.
HAZEL. Ho ho.
RUTHIE. That's a good one, Fred. Got anymore? (*To* SYLVIA.) A piece of advice from a girl who's old enough to be your—kid sister: good luck. You'll need it.
SYLVIA. (*To* GORMAN.) What does she mean by that?
GORMAN. (*To* RUTHIE.) Yeah, what do you mean by that?
RUTHIE. Oh, nothin'. (*To* SYLVIA.) Except, between you an' me, a girl could do better sleepin' with an electric blanket! (HAZEL *chuckles as she and* RUTHIE *cross to bar.*)
AGNES. (*Crosses* D. R.) Walter! Where are you?
WILLA. I wouldn't go in there if I were you, honey. That's the men's room. (WILLA *leads* AGNES *to table* R.) Why don't you come over here and relax, Mrs. Mitty, honey. That's your name, isn't it—Mrs. Mitty? I'll try to get Harry. (*Shouts.*) Harry! (*Almost a whisper as* HARRY *sticks his head out again.*) There's a Mrs. Mitty out here to see you.
HARRY. (*Enters, crosses to* AGNES.) Hi, Mrs. Mitty. Nice to see you. (*Then quickly crosses to* GORMAN.) Can I help you, Fred?
AGNES. I suggest you help me first. Where is Walter?
HARRY. Left about an hour ago to pick you up.
GORMAN. (*Crosses to* AGNES.) So you're the missus? I'm Fred Gorman, an old school chum of your husband's. (*To* HARRY.) Where is buddy boy hiding out?
WILLA. Cool it. Mr. Gorman. (*Indicates ladies room* U. R.)

(MITTY *enters* U. R. *wearing* WILLA's *coat, etc. He stops, looks into compact mirror, adjusts his kerchief. Satisfied, he puts compact into pocket.*)

MITTY. (*To* WILLA.) Hiya, Tiger. (*Crosses past* AGNES *toward door* U. L. *as others watch incredulously.*)

AGNES. Walter! (*He stops cold.*) What are you doing here? And looking like that? You're disgusting.

MITTY. (*Crosses to her, very calm.*) I am waiting for my husband!

AGNES. Walter, stop making a fool of yourself.

MITTY. Madam, you're drunk. (*Crosses past* GORMAN.)

GORMAN. Who the hell do you think you are, Walter?

MITTY. I'm the Welcome Wagon Hostess!

WILLA. (*Crosses to* MITTY.) She's telling the truth. She just welcomed me to the neighborhood. Come on, honey.

SYLVIA. This is like a regular show!

AGNES. I thought I braced myself for this moment, but all I can say is—

MITTY. (*Stops, turns. To others.*) Ssshhh, everybody, Agnes is going to make a speech—!

AGNES. (*Crosses to* MITTY.) You get out of those ridiculous clothes and come right home! I don't want any nonsense!

HARRY. This is your moment, Walt.

WILLA. Take advantage of it, Tiger.

AGNES. (*To* WILLA.) You keep out of this—you're a naughty woman!

WILLA. Well, we can't all be lucky.

HARRY. Stand up to her like a man.

MUSIC INTO #19

WILLA. Don't stand there, tell her—
AGNES. Tell me what, Walter?

YOU'RE NOT

MITTY.	BOYS and GIRLS.
Nice, you're not.	
Neat, you're not.	
Spice, you're not.	
Sweet, you're not.	
You take a spring day **and** chill it	
	Tell her off, Walt
Bad	
	Yeh
You are. Cold	
	Yeh

You are. Mad

        Yeh

You are. Old

        Yeh

You are.

You bake a doughnut and fill it.

        Right!

You're the "tic" in neurotic,
The "sigh" in psychotic,
The "dog" in dogmatic,
That's what.

        That's what!

But,

        But what?

Won—

        Yeh

derful, wil—

        Yeh

ling, ado—

        Yeh

rable, thril—

        Yeh

ling, enticing—
ly new

        Enticingly new

You're not!

MITTY.	BOYS and GIRLS.	AGNES.
	Chic	Walter
You're not.		
	Wit	Walter
You're not.		
	Meek	Walter
You're not.		
	Fit	Walter
You're not.		

AGNES.		BOYS and GIRLS.
You know the things I put up with		Shut her up, Walt!

MITTY.	BOYS and GIRLS.	AGNES.
	Tight	Walter
You are.		
	Thorn	Walter
You are.		
	Blight	Walter

You are.

	Worn	Walter

You are.

AGNES.	BOYS and GIRLS.
Champagne you don't fill my cup with	Yeah?
MITTY.	AGNES.
You're a great little nagger.	My best years I've
Your tongue is a dagger.	Given to you. What
A flair for complaining you've got, but	A crazy fool I've been.

MITTY.	BOYS and GIRLS.	AGNES.
Sen—		
	Yeh	Walter
sual, pas—		
	Yeh	Walter
sionate, sex		
	Yeh	Walter Mitty

With a dash in it . . .

MITTY, BOYS and GIRLS.
   Strictly entre nous . . .
AGNES.
   Strictly entre nous
MITTY.
   You're not.
AGNES.
   I'm not?
MITTY, BOYS and GIRLS.
   You're positively, absolutely, definitely, not!

(HARRY *lifts* MITTY's *arm in victory.* GROUP *applauds. Suddenly* AGNES *hits* MITTY *with her pocketbook, knocking him to floor.*)

SYLVIA. This is better than chop suey!

WILLA. Don't take that, Tiger. Now's the time to give her the "coup de Gracie." Show her.

AGNES. Show me what? What is she talking about? What else have you been up to, Walter?

MITTY. (*Rises, takes off coat and scarf, then removes papers from inside jacket pocket.*) She means these! They just have to be signed and I'm free: insurance, the broker's listing, my letter of resignation—I never knew a signature could be that important!

GORMAN. Don't kid yourself. It's the most important thing in the world. Take it from me.

MITTY. (*Crosses to bar, others follow.*) I'm going to sign them now in front of you, Agnes. In front of Thee!

AGNES. You wouldn't dare!

MITTY. (*Spreading papers on bar.*) Oh, I wouldn't, wouldn't I?

HARRY. Let me get you a pen, Walt.

MITTY. I got my own, thank you. (*Removes pen from pocket.*)

WILLA. Three times—Walter J. Mitty—and the world is yours!

MITTY. And yours, Willa. And yours! (*About to sign papers, hesitates.*)

WILLA. Then sign the papers.

SYLVIA. I think you're all nuts!

AGNES. Walter, I'm warning you—don't sign!

GORMAN. Go, Buddy Boy, go! Once you've done it, you'll feel great. I know!

AGNES. If you sign those I am going to have you put away. And I can, you know—I have mother as a witness. She agrees with me that you are mentally ill!

HARRY. Wait, think back: what were you like today before you met Willa? And remember what you said about that machine gun!

AGNES. Machine gun?

WILLA. Can't you see us having cocktails with the High Lama at the Taj Mahal, and flying to the Riviera for breakfast! And don't you want to see me do "Fan the Flame" at the Folies?

AGNES. Walter, you will end up in jail, I know it. All the years I've given you trying to keep you a good, honest husband and father, and now you've let these people ruin your entire future.

GORMAN. You've got no future if you don't sign. Trust me.

MITTY. (*Gazing at fountain pen.*) Peninnah's pen. Peninnah's pen— (*Looks at* WILLA, HARRY *and* GORMAN, *then turns to* AGNES, *hands her papers.*) Take me home, Agnes. I just want to go home . . .

SYLVIA. Gee, I never thought he'd do that!

MUSIC UP #20

(*The SCRIM closes, leaving* AGNES *and* MITTY *alone on stage.*)

AGNES. Walter, poor Walter. Men like you who have to make their own little dream world must have someone like me in order to get by from day to day. I'd like it to be different, but then it wouldn't be for your sake. I don't want it this way any more than you do. Where did it go wrong?

AGGIE (*Reprise.*)

AGNES.
> When it rained we waited for the rainbow,
> When it stormed we laughed, we joked.

But now when it rains, what happens, oh, Walter,
We get soaked!

Once I was your life, Walter, Walter, Walter,
Now I'm just your wife; oh darling, what happened?
Who's at fault?
Now it's "Agnes" and "Walter," but
Once it was "Aggie" and "Walt."

FAST SEGUE TO #21

LIGHTS FADE SLOWLY

ACT TWO

Scene 8

LIGHTS up on neighborhood street, the following morning.
PENINNAH *strolls down the aisle toward Stage.*

WALKIN' WITH PENINNAH (*Reprise.*)

PENINNAH.
   It's coke and lollies when I'm walkin' with my daddy,
   And who needs dollies when I'm walkin' with my daddy,
   No toy—or boy—could steal my heart away,
   When I'm walkin' with my daddy,
   Just me and my daddy,
   We're taking a walk today.

(*Sits on apron. SCRIM opens.*)

MUSIC OUT

LIGHTS DIM SLIGHTLY

ACT TWO

Scene 9

LIGHTS up on Mitty kitchen, a few seconds later.

AGNES. (*Enters* L., *crosses to imaginary window, opens it and calls out.*) Peninnah, come in from the front porch. Time for breakfast.

PENINNAH. Coming! (*Enters, crosses* L., *takes off coat.*)

AGNES. Where have you been?

PENINNAH. I was just walking and thinking about Daddy. What's wrong with him?

AGNES. Don't ask too many questions this morning, Peninnah.

PENINNAH. Is he sick?

AGNES. No, I wouldn't call it sick, Peninnah. Let's say he's having growing pains.

PENINNAH. (*Sits.* AGNES *serves breakfast.*) Growing pains? But he's a big man.

AGNES. Age doesn't have anything to do with it. Some people grow up faster than others. Your Daddy was a little slow, I'm afraid.

PENINNAH. I don't understand. Is Daddy sick because of something you did, Mommie?

AGNES. Something he did to himself, Peninnah, but Mommie's the medicine—the bad-tasting medicine—and some day that will all be clear to you.

PENINNAH. But he's going to get better, isn't he?

AGNES. Oh, yes. Once he understands that we love him and accepts the fact that he'll never be rich or famous—then the ice bag and the black coffee will do the rest.

PENINNAH. He looks awful. I peeked into his room and he looks awful.

AGNES. (*Calling out more gently than usual.*) Walter! Please hurry. Come to breakfast or you'll make us late for church and you'll be late for inventory. (MITTY *enters* U. R., *holding ice pack to head. There is a moment of awkward silence as they face each other.*)

MITTY. (*Trying to make the best of it.*) 'Morning, Agnes.

AGNES. (*Coldly.*) Good morning, Walter.

MITTY. (*Crosses to* PENINNAH.) 'Morning, Peninnah. (*Kisses her.*)

AGNES. (*Starts to correct him.*) Peni— (*Catches herself, puts hand to her mouth.*)

PENINNAH. 'Morning, Daddy. You all right?

MITTY. Fine, Peninnah, fine. (*Sticks tongue out.*) See! (*Sits.*)

AGNES. Have your coffee first, Walter. Then take your vitamins. Two green and one red.

PENINNAH. Daddy, do your growing pains hurt?

MITTY. My what?

PENINNAH. Mommy said you had growing pains.

MITTY. She did?

AGNES. Peninnah, go next door to Dorothy and borrow some milk.

MITTY. I take my coffee black, Agnes, you know that.

AGNES. No, Walter, it's for Peninnah's cereal.

PENINNAH. (*At kitchen cabinet, removes gift-wrapped package, crosses to* MITTY *and hands it to him.*) Here's the present I bought you, Daddy.

MITTY. Thank you, darling. (*Kisses her.*)

AGNES. Go, Peninnah—mind now. (PENINNAH *exits* L. *Another awkward silence.*) What have you got to say for yourself, Walter?

MITTY. I've been thinking, Agnes.

AGNES. So have I.

MITTY. About what happened to us, Agnes—

AGNES. *Us?* Don't bring me into this, Walter.

MITTY. I mean me, Agnes. Me.

AGNES. You passed out. You ruined my entire birthday dinner. I had to put you to bed. I wanted it to be so nice—just the family at home—and Peninnah and I sat here the whole evening—

MITTY. I know how embarrassed you were, coming into Harry's bar to get me—and seeing me with all those people—

AGNES. (*Surprised.*) *Me?* In Harry's Bar?

MITTY. Coming and finding me there like that, about to sign all those papers. I know how embarrassing it must have been—

AGNES. Walter, what are you talking about? Do you know what you're talking about? I never left the house all day yesterday after we got back, and neither did you!

MITTY. Neither did I? Agnes, we were both there! (*Puzzled.*) I even quit my job yesterday. Do you realize we're practically on welfare!

AGNES. Nonsense. I just spoke to Mr. MacMillan on the telephone and he told me to tell you not to be late for inventory.

MITTY. He did? But there was this girl—Willa de Wisp!

AGNES. Now that's ridiculous. Nobody is named Willa de Wisp!

MITTY. Are you—

AGNES. Walter, you've got to stop dreaming.

MITTY. Dreaming? (*Incredulous.*) It can't be!

AGNES. You've got to stop believing your own fantasies, Walter.

MITTY. Fantasies? What are you saying?

AGNES. Maybe we *should* see a doctor, Walter?

MITTY. But I was—you were— (*Gives up.*) Maybe we should. Agnes. Maybe we should . . .

PENINNAH. (*Enters* L., *carrying quart of milk.*) Oh, Daddy, it's so beautiful out. Can we make your birthday today?

MITTY. Huh? I guess after what your mother just told me, I don't see why not.

PENINNAH. And can we go to New York after?

MITTY. What do you want to do there?

PENINNAH. Eat at the Automat.

MITTY. It's a date, right after I'm through with Mr. MacMillan.

AGNES. Oh, and speaking of Mr. MacMillan, you'd better go up and shave or you'll·be late for inventory and you'll make us late for church. And you know there's nothing more embarrassing than walking into a church service after it's begun. And you know how ugly you look when you need a shave. And Mrs. MacMillan promised to propose our name for the Board of the Community Culture Center—

MITTY. All right, Agnes. All right! (*Crosses* U. R.)

AGNES. All I ask is that you hurry, Walter. It takes so little to be considerate. (*To* PENINNAH.) Peninnah, we don't sniffle at the table—go blow your nose!

LIGHTS FADE SLOWLY

ACT TWO

SCENE 10

LIGHTS up on Mitty bathroom upstairs. MITTY, U. R., *looks into imaginary mirror.*

MITTY. (*Half talking and half singing.*) By the time I'm *fifty* . . . (*To himself.*) 'Morning, Walter, you look rotten. I've never seen you look so terrible. But it's like you always said: you have to take the bad with the good. Einstein told you that . . . it's all relative. (*Considers.*) Tell you the truth, I don't think you look so ugly with a beard. It gives you a kind of distinguished caveman look. (*Thumps chest and gives Tarzan call.*)

AGNES. (*Offstage.*) Walter, are you all right?

MITTY. Yes, dear, I'm fine. (*Finds compact in shirt pocket, as* GORMAN, WILLA, HARRY *and* IRVING *enter* U. L.) It's Willa's compact! Agnes lied to me just now! She lied to me! (*After a thoughtful pause.*) No, Agnes lied *for* me! She didn't want me to be embarrassed and ashamed. She never wanted me to realize I might have failed if I signed all those papers! She knows I have a place and belong, and that *they* don't! I wonder how they are, Harry . . . Fred . . . Irving . . . Willa . . . ?

MUSIC UP #22

(*LIGHTS up dim on Harry's bar.*)

THE LONELY ONES

GORMAN.
   Hello, I love you, goodbye.
WILLA.
   I love singing, good healthy clinging,
IRVING.
   Willa, Willa
GORMAN.
   Hello, I love you, goodbye,
WILLA.
   I love dancing, crazy romancing,
IRVING.
   Willa, Willa

MUSIC CONTINUES UNDER DIALOGUE

MITTY. I wonder if they miss not having a home to go to—there's nothing sadder than being alone, and you're not alone, Walter. They have no one to ask them how they are or to see how they're feeling in the morning, or even anybody to lie for them. They just have themselves and that's not enough, is it, Walter? No, it's just not enough.

WILLA.	GORMAN.	IRVING.
Marriage is for old folks, old folks		
Marriage is for old folks, old folks, so	Hello, I love you Hello, I love you	Willa, Willa

GORMAN, WILLA, IRVING, HARRY.
   Goodbye!

   (*They exit* U. L. *LIGHTS fade on Harry's bar.*)

AGNES. (*Enters kitchen.*) Walter, I am going to back the car out. Peninnah and I are ready . . . close the door tightly behind you . . . and if you don't want to get fired, you'll move fast. (PENINNAH *enters. MUSIC UP. TAPOCKETA THEME #23.*
   AGNES. *and* PENINNAH *exit up house aisle.*)

   LIGHTS remain on MITTY

ACT TWO

SCENE 11 (*Epilogue*)

Scene segues into a repeat of original ACT 1 *Firing Squad dream.*

THE WALTER MITTY MARCH (*Reprise.*)

GROUP.
Mighty Mitty! You're hist'ry's shining light,
Walter Mitty! Hey man, you're out of sight!
MITTY. (*Repelling* MACMILLAN'S *attempt to tie his hands.*)
Sir! (MACMILLAN *tries to blindfold him.*) To hell with the hand-
kerchief!

(MACMILLAN *unfolds scroll and reads:*)

MACMILLAN. Walter Mitty, by my order, I, S.O.B. MacMillan,
your employer, have found you guilty as charged and hereby
sentence you to be shot. Would you like a cigarette? (*Offers
cigarette.* MITTY *shakes head "no," coughs and points to congested chest.*) Have you any last request?
MITTY. If you don't mind, I'd like to give the final command
myself.
MACMILLAN. As you wish. (*They shake hands.*) Good luck,
Mitty.
MITTY. Thank you. (*Addressing Squad.*) Ready! Aim! Fire!

(*A loud REPORT.* MITTY *clutches his heart dramatically.
DRUM roll out on shot. MUSIC UP--#23 cont'd.—ad lib
as the* SQUAD *and* PEASANT WOMEN *exit L.* [*MUSIC OUT.*]
He discovers WILLA'S *compact in breast pocket, opens it and
the "bullets" fall to the floor. He then bursts into a fit of
triumphant laughter, abruptly interrupted by:*)

AGNES. Walter!

MUSIC #24

THE SECRET LIFE (*Reprise.*)

AGNES. (*Crosses down aisle.*) Walter! Walter J. Mitty. I just knew I'd have to come back to call you. Peninnah and I are sitting in the car and it's freezing out just like I said it would	CHORUS. (*Offstage, softly under dialogue.*) When the world seems hard to bear,

. . . come out the front door and lock it behind you.

MITTY. (*Crosses downstairs, into kitchen.*) Coming, Agnes, I'm coming.

AGNES. Peninnah filled your pen. Take it with you for your inventory . . . it's on the kitchen table.

MITTY. (*Picks up pen.*) I got it, Agnes.

AGNES. And bring the book of commutation tickets for the toll booth if you're planning on driving into New York today.

MITTY. Yes, dear, I will.

AGNES. Because we can't afford any extra money this month . . . I've got to pay the Blue Cross first thing in the morning—

MITTY. (*Picking up book.*) I got it, Agnes!

AGNES. Be careful of the dog's water bowl . . . Wednesday morning you tripped over it and the poor thing almost died from thirst.

MITTY. (*Avoiding it.*) I see it, Agnes!

(*During above dialogue,* MITTY *has moved Downstage, gathering his hat and coat.*)

AGNES. And don't wear the tie with the stain on it.

MITTY. I won't, dear. It's O.K.

(MITTY *puts on coat, goes out through imaginary front door Down Center, stops, turns back to door, locks it.*)

You can dream a dream,

And suddenly you're there,
In the secret life, the secret life.

Time goes by against your will,

But just a dream away,

Time is standing still

In the secret life,

AGNES. What's holding you up, Walter? My God, you'll never change!

(MITTY *stands at "door" for a moment. A smile breaks across his face as he strides determinedly up Center aisle.*)

MITTY. I'm coming, Aggie . . . I'm coming!

The secret life!

TENOR. (*Offstage.*)
From earthbound to boundless you fly,
Tall, proud and free,
To be all you long to be!
    CHORUS. (*Offstage.*)
And who's to know,
And who's to say
Which world is really real,
The world of every day,
Or the secret life, the secret life,
The wonderful, magical, glorious,
Secret
Life!

CURTAIN

THE END

SET PLOT

The scenery may be as elaborate, or as simple, as desired.

The show, as originally produced in New York, had only one basic set which served the entire needs of the play. Briefly, the changes of scenes or locales were effected through the use of lights, *periaktoi*, a platform, and a "kitchen cabinet" that converted into a bar by means of a track in the floor.

The transitions into the dream sequences were realized through the use of lighting, a motorized, overhead revolving mirror ball, and the musical "tapocketa" theme. All became operative a few seconds before each dream sequence.

Following is a detailed outline of the set plot:

The nature of the original set is a single unit consisting of a platform extending across half the upstage area; a dark scrim behind the platform, and a cyc about a foot behind the scrim, with a ground row between the cyc and scrim. Two *periaktoi* (3 sided revolving flats) flank the platform, with steps from stage to platform immediately instage of each *periaktoi*. There is a crossover behind the cyc.

On the stage level, a bar-sink unit sits center stage in a single track. This unit swivels in the track and doubles as sink on one side and bar on the other. Storage bins for glasses, bottles and costumes are under the right-to-center edge of the platform.

Stage R. *periaktoi* has plugs of:

1. Harry's Bar (window as seen from inside the bar, covered in black scrim).
2. Space Dream (space ship).
3. Folies de Mitty (Billboard).

Stage L. *periaktoi* has plugs of:

1. Mitty Kitchen Window (Venetian blind and two geraniums on the sill).
2. Harry's Bar (Juke box, covered in black scrim).

Coat hooks are attached on the on-stage frames of both *periaktoi*.

ACT ONE

Scene 1:
PROLOGUE
Platform: Chest of drawers center.
Lower Stage: Sink flush against platform. Breakfast table at
    s. L. with 3 chairs (backless stools which double in bar
    scenes).
s. L. *Periaktoi:* Jukebox (covered with black scrim).
s. R. *Periaktoi:* Rocket Ship.

Scene 2:
Kitchen: Same as Prologue.
s. R. *Periaktoi:* Same as Prologue.
s. L. *Periaktoi:* Kitchen window plug.

Scene 3:
SPACE DREAM
Same as Scene 2.
s. R. *Periaktoi:* Rocket ship plug.
s. L. *Periaktoi:* Same.

Scene 4:
KITCHEN
Same as Scene 2.

Scene 5:
SURGICAL DREAM
No change. (Preset white kitchen utensils s. R. wing.)

Scene 6:
KITCHEN
Same as Scene 2.

Scene 7:
FAMILY CAR
Three stools set in front of closed scrim.

Scene 8:
HARRY'S BAR
Platform—cleared.
Lower Stage: Bar unit angled to platform. Kitchen table now
    covered with checkered cloth. 3 bar stools.
Table s. R. with checkered cloth and four stools.
s. R. *Periaktoi:* Harry's Bar plug, lit.
s. L. *Periaktoi:* Juke Box plug, lit.

Scene 9:
PLAYBOY PENTHOUSE DREAM
No change.

Scene 10:
HARRY'S BAR
Same as Scene 8.
Lower Stage: No change.

s. R. *Periaktoi:* No change.
s. R. *Periaktoi:* No change.
Scene 11:
  BAR
    Same as Scene 8.
Scene 12:
  VARIOUS OFFICES AND HOMES IN WATERBURY
    No change. Area lighting only.

ACT TWO

Scene 1:
  HARRY'S BAR
    Same as Act I, Scene 8.
Scene 2:
  FOLIES DE MITTY DREAM
    Platform: Cleared.
    Lower Stage: Bar flush against platform. Tables and stools
      as set before.
    s. R. *Periaktoi:* Folies de Mitty plug—lit.
    s. R. *Periaktoi:* Juke Box plug—dark.
Scene 3:
  HARRY'S BAR
    Same as Act I, Scene 8.
Scene 4:
  STEAM ROOM AND HARRY'S BAR
    Platform: Small area U. R. lit with stool. No other changes.
Scene 5:
  HARRY'S BAR
    Same as Act I, Scene 8.
Scene 6:
  PSYCHIATRIST DREAM
    Platform: One stool c. "SUPPORT MENTAL HEALTH"
      sign U. S. C.; 2 Thurberesque drawings.
    Lower Stage: Stools arranged in semi-circle. No other
      changes.
Scene 7:
  HARRY'S BAR
    Same as Act I, Scene 8.
Scene 8:
  FRONT OF MITTY'S HOUSE
    Scrim closed.
Scene 9:
  MITTY KITCHEN
    Same as Act I, Scene 2. (Exception: Preset black covered
      table and stool s. R. area.)

Scene 10:

MITTY BATHROOM AND HARRY'S BAR

No changes, but Harry will angle bar-sink unit strictly for "The Lonely Ones."

Scene 11:

EPILOGUE

Same as Prologue.

COSTUME PLOT

ACT ONE

Scene 1:

MITTY: Shorts, undershirt, socks, shoes.

PEASANT WOMEN: Gray shrouds, black head scarves.

SOLDIERS: Helmet liner, black shirt, tie and trousers, black socks and shoes.

MACMILLAN: Same as soldiers, except: Officer's hat with unique insignia.

Scene 2:

AGNES: Blue dress, beige shoes, apron, blue hat, green raincoat, scarf, pocketbook, gloves.

PENINNAH: Green dress, light blue blouse, hat, coat, scarf, light blue tights.

MITTY: Grey herringbone suit, beige fly-front raincoat, grey hat, dress shirt, stained non-maroon tie, maroon tie.

Scene 3:

MITTY: Elaborate space helmet.

MACMILLAN: Olive drab raincoat, soldier costume from Act I, Scene 1.

Scene 4:

Same as Act I, Scene 2.

Scene 5:

DOCTORS: White surgeon trousers, jacket, cap, sneakers.

NURSES: White surgeon gown cap, mask, sneakers.

MACMILLAN (*Patient*): White hospital gown, cap, rubber shower clogs.

MITTY: White surgeon gown over costume from Act I, Scene 4.

Scene 6:

Same as Act I, Scene 2.

Scene 7:

Same as Act I, Scene 2.

Scene 8:

HARRY: White shirt, black bow tie, black pants, white waist apron, red vest, black shoes and socks.

MITTY: Same as Act I, Scene 2.

WILLA: Blue dress, fur-lined raincoat (reversed), beige pocketbook, pink high heeled shoes, pink scarf.

IRVING: Tan boots, blue turtleneck sweater, tan sport jacket, grey pants, motorcycle goggles.

GORMAN: Black pants, tie and vest, hounds-tooth black and white sport jacket, checked sport hat, black raincoat, black shoes and socks, white shirt.

HAZEL: Black low-cut dress with grey ostrich feather collar, red satin and velvet cape, pink high heeled shoes, flower in hair, red pocketbook, pink gloves, auburn wig.

RUTHIE: Green sequined dress, green high heeled shoes, green satin, fur-collared jacket, green purse.

Scene 9:

MITTY: Gold brocade smoking jacket over Act I, Scene 2 costume.

HARRY: Red waiter's jacket over Act I, Scene 8 costume.

CREPE SUZETTE: Orchid wig, pink chiffon negligee with black ostrich trim over pink ruffled bra and panties, pink shoes.

TORTONI: Black wig, red satin skirt, black lace-trimmed blouse, pink shoes, over black and red lace bra and panties.

APPLE TURNOVER: Pink wig, black horn-rimmed glasses, black and white checked 2-piece suit, over pink bra and panties with black polka dots, pink shoes and scarf.

BAKLAVA (AGNES): Very brief pink chiffon "Salome" outfit with seven chiffon veils or panels, individually tucked into costume for each performance, long magenta head scarf.

Scene 10:

Same as Act I, Scene 8.

Scene 11:

MITTY: Same as Act I, Scene 10.

HARRY: Same as Act I, Scene 10.

WILLA: Same as Act I, Scene 10.

4 BOYS: Regular business suits.

ADELAIDE: Grey maid's dress with white collar, cuffs, hat,

2 GIRLS:

    a. Beige dress, shoes.

    b. Black and white checked dress with yellow blouse.

AGNES: Same as Act I, Scene 7, plus hairnet, curlers, plastic protective sheet.

ACT TWO

Scene 1:

HAZEL: Hat and coat off.

RUTHIE: Hat and coat off.

HARRY: Same as Act I, Scene 8.

MITTY: Same as Act I, Scene 10 (hat and coat on).

WILLA: Same as Act I, Scene 10 (hat and coat on).

Scene 2:

MITTY: Black cape and slouch hat over Act II, Scene 1 costume.

WILLA: Black brocade grown, red boa.

MALE DANCERS: Black shirt, red bow tie, black pants, red vest.

GORMAN: Top hat, black raincoat over regular costume.

HAZEL: Same as Act I, Scene 8 without cape, with sheer black coat.

RUTHIE: Same as Act I, Scene 8, with sheer black coat.

HARRY: Red brocade waiter's jacket with black sequined lapel and cuffs, black pants, white shirt.

IRVING (*Waiter*): Black pants, red and black striped vest, white shirt, black bow tie, tan boots.

CUSTOMERS: Ordinary street clothes.

Scene 3:

Same as Act I, Scene 12.

Scene 4:

HARRY: Same as Act I, Scene 12.

MITTY: Same as Act I, Scene 12.

WILLA: Same as Act I, Scene 12.

IRVING: Large bath towel around waist, small bath towel around shoulders (bare chest).

Scene 5:

Same as Act II, Scene 4.

Scene 6:

MITTY: Same as Act II, Scene 4.

AGNES: Blue dress, pocketbook.

ARTIST: Red beret, pink smock, fake beard with ear bandage.

JUVENILE DELINQUENT: Blue T-shirt, blue jeans, black boots, wide black belt, motorcycle fancy hat.

NYMPHOMANIAC: Fur coat over red crepe dress.

OTHERS: Ordinary street clothes.

Scene 7:

MITTY: Same as Act II, Scene 4.

WILLA: Same as Act II, Scene 4.

HARRY: Same as Act II, Scene 4.

MALE CUSTOMERS: Suits.

FEMALE CUSTOMERS: Dresses.

SYLVIA: Blonde wig, gold satin coat over gold satin sheath.

GORMAN: Same as Act I, Scene 8.

Scene 8 and 9:

PENINNAH: Same as Act I, Scene 2, except blue plaid dress replaces green dress (coat, hat, scarf on).

AGNES: Red dress, coat, hat, scarf, pocketbook.

MITTY: Same as Act I, Scene 2.

Scene 10:

WILLA: Pink lace dress.

HARRY: Same as Act II, Scene 2.

GORMAN: Same as Act I, Scene 8.

IRVING: Same as Act I, Scene 8.

Scene 11:

Same as Act I, Scene 1, except MITTY: Suit, pants, shirt, no tie.

MASTER PROP LIST

ACT I—*Pre-set:*
3 rifles on fire exit stairs.
Upstage Right Table:
    Razor, towel, hammer, 2 bottle champagne (Ginger ale).
Wall behind S. R. *Periaktoi:*
    Table with bar tablecloth, 3 stools stacked.
Black drape over space ship in S. R. Periaktoi.

Hung in Downstage Right wing:
    Exaggerated surgeon's knife, spatula, eggbeater, thread spool.
Hung in S. R. *Wing:*
    Black masking cloth for bar table.
On Kitchen Unit: (Kitchen facing audience)
    Coffee pot with mixed instant coffee.
    Potholder.
    Frying pan with two plastic fried eggs.
    Spatula.
    Cup, saucer, spoon.
    Dinner plate.
    Mixing bowl with eggbeater and fork.
    2 cereal bowls with one spoon.
    Box of Rice Krispies (inner wax paper removed).
    Salt and pepper shakers (empty).
    3 folded napkins.
    Knife and fork.
    2 orange juice glasses.
    Bar cloth and dish towel hung in towel ring.
In S. R. *Kitchen Unit Shelf:*
    Box of napkins.
    Harry's green ballpoint pen.
In S. L. *Kitchen Unit Shelf:*
    Bottle of vitamins.
    Peninnah's pencil in gift box.
In Refrigerator Unit S. L.:
    Bar tablecloth.
    Milk container with water.
    Orange juice bottle with mixed Tang.
    Black ribbon bow with hairpin.
    Empty butter dish.
    2 hardboiled eggs.
    Book of commutation tickets with pen.
On S. L. *Kitchen Table:*
    Kitchen tablecloth.
    Ashtray.

Three stools on marks at kitchen table.
Three bar stools in bar unit niches.
Dresser (reversed) up center of platform.

In s. r. *Bar Bin Below Platform:*
  All bar glasses, including: Brandy Alexander, Bloody Mary glasses.

In s. l. *Bar Bin Below Platform:*
  Harry's waiter jacket underneath.
  Mitty's smoking jacket with 2 cigarettes and matches in left pocket.
Under Platform: (Reading from s. r. to s. l.)
  Sealed bottle of beer.
  Bottle tray with:
    2 bottles Vodka (water).
    1 bottle Scotch (tea).
    1 bottle Rye (tea).
    1 bottle Bourbon (tea).
    Cocktail shaker, glass with cocktail straws and bottle opener.
    1 open beer bottle (with cap on, but loose).
  Bar tray with 4 ashtrays, 10-12 cocktail napkins, book of matches.
  Waste bucket with 2-3 inches water.

Prop Room Off Left:
  MacMillan's rope and blindfold.
  Bouquet of flowers.
  5 Princess telephones.
  4 regular telephones.
  Peninnah's workbook with pencil.
  MacMillan's earphones and microphone.
  Aggie's 2 Reader's Digests.
  Surgical tray with:
    Sheet,
    Hypodermic,
    Knife,
    Chest plate,
    Paint brush,
    Accordion with anesthetizer.
  Black leatherette stool.
  Jar of honey with comb.
White wooden stool in crossover.

MITTY:
 Pack of cigarettes and matches.
 Pen and comb.
 Ice pack.
 Compact with 3 screws inside (must be retrieved at end of each performance).
 Keys.
 Broker's listing and other papers.
WILLA:
 Pack of cigarettes and matches.
 Cigarette holder.
 Compact in pocketbook.
PENINNAH:
 Doll.
GORMAN:
 Cigars, matches, money.
ACT II—*Pre-Set:*
In Upstage Right Table:
 Telephone.
On Upstage Right Platform: (Just Downstage of curtain)
 Wooden stool.
 Bar tray with 3 champagne glasses.
Bar stool Downstage left under telephone.
Bouquet of flowers Upstage of bar stool.
2 bar stools in *outer* bar unit niches.
1 orange stool in prop room.
Black leatherette stool becomes Upstage stool of Scene 3 at S. R. table.
Kitchen tablecloth moves to top of refrigerator unit.
2 glasses with water, ashtray, and bar tablecloth on bar table.
Clear top of bar unit.
In Sink Compartment of Bar Unit: (Bar facing audience.)
 Box of vitamins.
 Glass with water.
 Coffee pot.
 Potholder.
 2 folded napkins.
 2 cups and saucers.
 2 spoons.
 1 cereal bowl.
 1 spoon.
 Box of Rice Krispies.
 2 orange juice glasses.
S. R. Periaktoi turned to Folies de Mitty.
S. L. Periaktoi turned to Bar.

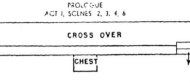

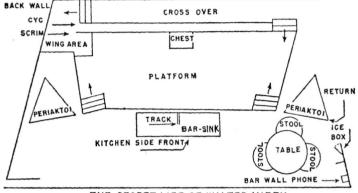

THE SECRET LIFE OF WALTER MITTY

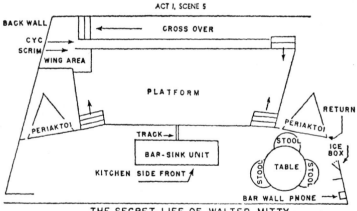

THE SECRET LIFE OF WALTER MITTY

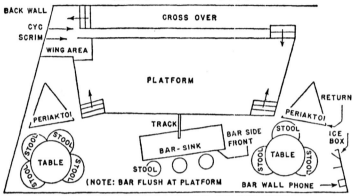

THE SECRET LIFE OF WALTER MITTY

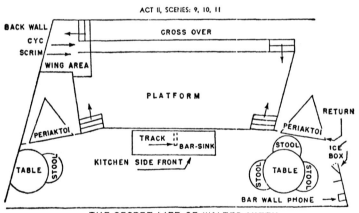

THE SECRET LIFE OF WALTER MITTY

RENTAL MATERIALS

An orchestration consisting of **Piano/Conductor Score, Flute/Piccolo, Clarinet/Alto Saxophone 1, Clarinet/Alto Saxophone 2, Trumpet 1, Trumpet 2, Trombone, Percussion (Trumpet, Bells, Drums), Violins I & 2 (2 books), Viola, Cello, Bass, Harp** will be loaned two months prior to the production ONLY on the receipt of the Licensing Fee quoted for all performances, the rental fee and a refundable deposit. Please contact Samuel French for perusal of the music materials as well as a performance license application.

MUSIC USE NOTE

Licensees are solely responsible for obtaining formal written permission from copyright owners to use copyrighted music in the performance of this play and are strongly cautioned to do so. If no such permission is obtained by the licensee, then the licensee must use only original music that the licensee owns and controls. Licensees are solely responsible and liable for all music clearances and shall indemnify the copyright owners of the play(s) and their licensing agent, Samuel French, against any costs, expenses, losses and liabilities arising from the use of music by licensees. Please contact the appropriate music licensing authority in your territory for the rights to any incidental music.

IMPORTANT BILLING AND CREDIT REQUIREMENTS

If you have obtained performance rights to this title, please refer to your licensing agreement for important billing and credit requirements.